Starchasers:

A home Among the stars

By Kay Hawkins

Starchasers: A Home Among The Stars

Kay Hawkins

Published by Polilaudanum Press

Copyright 2019

First Edition 2019

ISBN: 978-0-9959794-9-9

Polilaudanum Press

Dedication

To Luke Maynard
Your continuing love and support
gets my further and further
every year.
Per ardua ad astra

Chapter 1

Skyler sat in his temporary captain's chair one last time. He stared at the screen that was showing them the view from outside. *Finally going home, back to Earth.* He watched the stars pass by. Space looked so different in person. It wasn't rainbow gas clouds up here. Space was like looking up at the night sky and being surrounded by it. The planets were closer, and the stars were brighter. *This is it, third year beings. I hope they don't send me to the frontlines. I don't have the experience to be a captain yet and I would hate to work at some remedial job.* He got up out of his chair and made his way off the bridge with no explanation.

Kax turned the controls over to autopilot and followed Skyler. She called out, "Skyler, where do you think you are going?"

He hit a button on the wall, and it opened a sliding door. "I'm going to my quarters, I need
to be alone."

She followed him into the room. "I'm confused, I thought you were excited to be going home?"

Skyler flopped down on his bed. "I am, it's the war that is bothering me. You do realize my father was killed at the end of the last Cassiopaean war?"

She sat down on the edge of the bed. "Skyler, as much as people say you look like your father, you are not him. You're too suborn to let the Cass kill you."

4

He scoffed. "Even if that were the truth, why am I going home? Earth is the place being attacked, so I have a higher risk of dying and I got no one waiting for me. Maybe it's a bad idea for me to go back there. You at least have a father. Good for you."

She rubbed her hand on his back. "You got Cane, right? He's got to count for something."

Skyler buried his head further into his pillow. "Go back to the bridge and let me have a few moments alone."

She tussled his blonde hair slightly, before getting up and leaving the room.

***

Michael's mind was full of worries. He sat there staring at the blinking lights on the control board in engineering. *This is it, finally going back to Earth. Going to pick up my diploma and officially graduate.* He made a fist. *So, what if I have invented things, and did this secret mission? They are going to send me to the engineering room on the frontlines, that is what they do to all the young Squallite. My dad is finally getting better and now I am going to die.* He groaned. *I guess it is better than living right now. Once word gets out, I stole the worm orb no Squallite will want to talk to me.* He banged his head on the desk. *I guess I'll just have to enjoy my time with my dad as much as I can.*

Chapter 2

Skyler watched as Kax landed the ship carefully. The day trip back was quicker than he remembered. *It's the beginning of the end,* Skyler thought. The ship landed, and all was silent. The crew stepped out of the doors of the ship. There was no one there but the one and only Fleet Admiral Cane.

Cane smiled at the crew once they were out of the ship and said, "You have been a very brave crew these last few months. I know you have many questions, all will be answered in time. Right now, I would like you to all follow me, your families are waiting outside."

As they walked out the doors their looks of despair turned to smiles as they saw their families once again. It had been a long time for some. One by one, Skyler watched the members of the crew run to go and greet their families.

Kax didn't hesitate to run up and gave her dad a big hug.

Michael made his way to the back of the crowd, towards an aged Squallite in a wheelchair.

Skyler scanned the crowd, there was no one there for him. He wasn't going to let it bother him. He knew how his mother was and hoped that she wouldn't come.

Kax waved Skyler over. "Hey Skyler, don't stand there alone. Come over here and meet my dad."

Skyler went over and shook the male Catillion's hand. "So, you're the father I hear so much about. Hello, Kax speaks very highly of you. I'm Skyler and might I say you have a very lovely daughter."

He nodded his head. "The name's David, and you must be the boy who dreams of being a captain like your father and is friends with my daughter?"

"I see my reputation proceeds me." Skyler brushed back his blonde hair. "And for now, yes. Me and your daughter are just friends."

Kax frowned while Skyler chuckled.

David narrowed his eyes at Skyler, "You do know Kax's mother was in the forces. Maybe I know who your father was, what was his name?"

Skyler smiled with pride. "Capitan Levi Therris, he died in the war when I was five."

David frowned, "Therris, you're Therris' kid?"

Skyler raised an eyebrow in confusion. "Yes, is there something wrong, sir?"

David was about to say something when a woman in a Grey uniform came up to the side of them. She grabbed Skyler's shoulder, pulling him towards her. "Skyler there you are I was looking for you. Didn't you see me?"

Shit, not my mother, ugh. Skyler turned and stared at his mother with a look of terror. "Well, there are so many people it was hard to notice anybody. I just thought I would come meet my friend Kax's dad."

She looked at David and then at Kax, "Your mother use to be a pilot, right? Her name was Carmen Tilly or something?"

Kax smiled. "Tillion, her name was Karmantha Tillion and yes she was."

Sandy snarled. "Yes, I remember her." She then looked at Skyler, "Come on now, we have to get going." She eyed David. "And David, keep your daughter away from my son."

David scoffed, "They're adults and not our former spouses. They can do what they want."

She grabbed onto Skyler's hand and pulled him like a child away from the rest of the group.

He pulled his arm back. "What was that all about? Why did you take me away? Kax is my friend. That was rude!" Skyler snapped at his mother.

She glared at Skyler. "Stop seeing that girl, she is nothing but trouble. Also, I talked to Fleet Admiral Davis. She said that the school will give you a letter of recommendation, for any college or job you want, when you leave the forces."

He stepped back and glared. "Why in the world would I ever leave the forces?"

His mother glared back. "Don't give me that tone. You should know by now that there is a war going on. You just came back from being stranded on a stinking planet for four months and now you want to stay in here? You're eighteen years old and I will not have you out gallivanting around space, getting yourself killed."

"I wasn't stranded. I signed up for the mission." The rage built in his eyes. He searched around. "This is my life. I want to be in space. I want to fight this war. I want to protect Earth. I don't want a government job or to be a labor worker. I want to go to space and make a difference! Can we please talk about this somewhere more private?"

"No, because the only place we are going is home to be with me and your father!" She snapped right back.

His upper lip twitched. "Charles is not my father! He's some asshole you married! I'm not leaving this academy and I'm twenty years old mother. Maybe if you paid attention to what was going on all these years, I wouldn't have been forced to live with Uncle Justin." He turned away and didn't look back.

"Fine, walk away! You're just like your father, you don't listen to anyone!" She yelled out. "Die alone, in space. See if I care, you ungrateful brat! Enjoy your fun with your feline whore!"

He clenched his fists, stopped in his tracks. He turned around and shouted not able to control himself. "Kax isn't a whore, she's the most decent woman I know!" But his mother was gone. He sighed. *First time she mentions my father to me in years and it's to insult me.* He pushed through the crowd and tried to get away as fast as he could. *I just want to be alone.* As soon as he placed his hand to open the door and step outside, O'Brien walked in. He stepped back.

"Hey there, lad, what's wrong?" It was obvious O'Brien could see the tears forming in Skyler's eyes.

Skyler was trying not to cry. "My mother is an uncaring bitch."

O'Brien gave Skyler a burly hug. "Don't say that, just because she didn't come."

Skyler scoffed. "Oh, she came. She just wants me to quit and get a government job, with my stepfather."

O'Brien cringed and let go, holding Skyler's shoulders. "Wait, your mother is here?"

Skyler sniffled. "Ya, she's over there somewhere in the grey uniform." He pointed in the distance.

O'Brien tried to look through the crowd. "She's coming this way." He panicked and said to Skyler. "Come on, lad, let's not worry about this. Let us go celebrate your home and head to the bar and have a drink."

Why would she be coming back? Skyler scratched his head. "Ya, sounds like a good idea."

Skyler went with O'Brien to the academy bar, hoping to chug a few beers and just relax. When they walked in, they noticed there were many others who had the same idea. The bar was full and overcrowded. O'Brien looked around the bar and back at Skyler. "You don't mind if we just take off to the city? I know a good Ol' Irish pub. It's just because this place is, well, you know."

Skyler nodded. "Ya, no problem, let's get out of here."

The two headed off to the parking garage. O'Brien's car was an old beat-up blue hover minivan.

Skyler looked at it in confusion. "I thought captains made more money than to drive an outdated minivan?"

Shrugging he answered, "We do, but I guess Emily took the Lexus again, so we're stuck with this. Trust me, it's almost as old as you. It's one of the first good working hover cars with the reusable jets."

There was nothing wrong with the van. Skyler he had never seen one of his teacher's cars before. He wasn't sure what to expect. They got in and drove off. Skyler kept an eye out, so he could memorize the scene and know the way if he ever wanted to visit this place on his own.

O'Brien shifted in the driver's seat. "Hey, you don't mind if I play some old Celtic music, do you?"

Skyler lightly snorted and nodded. "I have never met anyone who is as much of an Irish stereotype."

O'Brien laughed. "I know I'm bad, I just love my Irish heritage, never really thought about it. I know my daughter Emily doesn't really care, my sons are fifty-fifty about it."

Skyler shrugged. "I don't mind. I don't have much of a cultural heritage even if my last name is sort of Welsh."

Looking at his passenger. "Really? Welsh, I never knew where that name came from, to begin with. It's not that common."

Skyler nodded in agreement. "My dad was an only child and I don't think he had any cousins. I have never met anyone on his side and my grandparents are dead."

They soon got to the bar, a rustic old-fashioned Irish pub with a green neon-colored sign that read O'Shea. Inside the pub was hardwood with a full bar on the wall, clean bar stools and a lovely light and dark wood checkered pattern on the floor. The green, well-used countertops of the bar were the perfect place for O'Brien and Skyler tonight.

Skyler felt comfortable in this bar, even though he had never been in it before. O'Brien ordered them two pints. Skyler sighed and put his head down on the bar.

The drinks came, O'Brien picked up his. "Let's toast to your safe arrival home."

He let out a sigh of relief, smiled and picked up his beer to toast his elder. He took a sip, but O'Brien downed half a pint in one gulp.

He looked at Skyler. "Listen, I know you're upset about a few things but that's not what this is about. Tonight, we put that all behind and drink till we don't remember who you are. Because tonight, the stars are for looking at, not going to."

Skyler downed his pint and smiled. He missed nights like this. Finally, back on his home planet, this was a night to put aside his worries about his mother, school and the current war. His mind was worry free. The drinks kept coming.

Starting to feel the buzz, he realized that he hadn't said a word. A stabbing pain in his chest came when he tried to speak. There were so many emotions in the air. He was relaxed in one way but still mad, angry and stressed. He wanted to enjoy the night, but it had been so long since he had been on Earth. He wanted to enjoy this short moment in time. In the past year he had faced his own mortality, professed his love to Kax and she stomped on his heart. He thought he could handle this, but he was starting to doubt everything he knew. He was happy to have returned to Earth but seeing his mother brought back all the pain from his past, all the things he hoped to forget about his adolescence. He finished his beer and stared at the foam at the bottom of the empty glass.

O'Brien put his arm around Skyler, holding him tight. "Come on kid you have barely said a word since we got here. Now I told you if you're worried or upset to put that behind you tonight. This is a night of celebration."

Skyler took a deep sigh. "I think that's what I have been doing Captain, and I'm not sure I can do it anymore."

O'Brien patted Skyler on the back. "We have all been there, Laddie. You know I once dated your mother."

Skyler's heart stopped and his eyes bugged out as he turned to look at O'Brien. Not believing what he just heard he spit out, "No, you didn't. I know the list of guys she dated and you're not on it!"

O'Brien was taken back by Skyler's harsh response and nodded back. "Well then your list isn't up to date. I dated her before your father. She was in the academy and I was young, just starting my career with a full head of bright red curls. I was quite charming. She was a young cute attractive brunette when I asked her out. She wasn't shy and said yes. I don't know what your dad saw in her, but she was so bossy. She ordered for me and she had so many strict rules about when and how I could touch her. Let's just say there wasn't a second date and I have tried to avoid her since, she was just weird to me."

Cane had come in sometime during O'Brien's story and was listening from nearby. Standing next to Skyler on the right, he frowned at O'Brien. "You never dated Sandy, if you are going to tell a story to cheer him up, don't tell him a fake one."

Skyler jerked around in his seat to look at Cane who was in casual clothes, a pair of dark denim jeans and a light tan dress shirt. He could barely remember the last time he saw Cane so dressed down.

Cane looked at the empty glasses on the table and then at Skyler. "O'Brien tried to date your mom, he bugged her and bugged her to go out for dinner and when she agreed, he stiffed her with the bill. Your mother is good at holding grudges and still wants to be paid back for the dinner."

Skyler turned his head slowly and narrowed his eyes at O'Brien. "Is that true?"

With a face as red as a plum tomato and, he nodded. Letting out a huge sigh not being able to compete with two sets of hawk eyes he admitted defeat. "Cane is telling the truth. I was broke and it was a thing I use to do when I was young, go out with girls and stiff them. Your mom is the only one still trying to collect."

O'Brien looked at the bar then at Cane. "Hey, do you think that maybe since I will be paying for these drinks Sandy will count it as part of the money I owe her?"

Cane rubbed his temples. "Oh, ya any mother would encourage her son's teacher to contribute to her son's alcoholism."

The bartender came to the bar and started picking up the glasses in front of them. As she leaned down exposing her cleavage in her black unbuttoned dress top, she asked, "Can I get you boys anything else?"

Cane shook his head. "No, we're just about to get going, thank you, though. Our friend here will be paying the bill." Cane took Skyler by the arm and pointed to O'Brien.

Skyler, a little buzzed, got off the stool with Cane.

Cane took Skyler out of the bar, quickly walking him to his cherry red hovercar.

Annoyed that Cane was being so pushy, he pushed Cane off. "Stop it! I can walk on my own, you're not my father!"

Cane stopped dead in his tracks, looked at Skyler's green eyes and then at the ground in regret. "Your right, I'm not, I'm sorry I shouldn't be pushing you into any of this. If you don't want to come, you don't have to."

Skyler rubbed his forehead seeing the hurt look in Cane's eyes. "I'm sorry. I didn't mean it like that. I did want to get out of there but, not so fast. My heads a little light."

Cane looked at Skyler's sad eyes. "I wanted to be your father. I never had any children of my own."

He looked at Cane's serious eyes. He gave Cane a hug. "Life has not dealt us fair hands, has it."

Cane hugged back and ruffled Skyler's hair. "Come on kid, let's get you home."

Skyler let go and looked up at the stars. "I can't, I don't have a place to go to unless my old room is available. But, if I had a choice I would want to go someplace where I could see the stars."

Nodding his head, he hit the unlock button on his keys and got in. "Come on Skyler, let's get in the car. I know a place we can go."

Skyler opened the door and stepped into the passenger side of the red convertible hover-car. He sat on the tan leather seats and did up his seatbelt.

Cane turned the car on and started driving them out of the bar's parking lot.

Skyler looked at the glowing blue lights on the dashboard. He reached his hand out to hit the button to change the radio station.

Cane moved Skyler's hand away. "No touching my controls, I have everything set to the way I like it. Don't touch the temperature, stereo and even the volume that's my rules. Everything else is fine."

Skyler looked at Cane confused. "Really? You're that anal about the radio? No wonder you aren't married. In my experience, it's best to let the chicks play with the radio. It makes them feel more relaxed."

"How I like my car has nothing to do with why I'm not married." Cane frowned.

Skyler took a long awkward pause. "So why are you single?"

Cane took a deep breath. "Long story but mostly I have had one too many broken hearts."

Puzzled, Skyler stared at Cane. "Did my mother break your heart?"

Cane almost stopped the car, he tensed up. There was a sadness forming in his eyes. "Yes, she did, but she was not the only one. There was another before her, and one after. But your mom found ways to break it repeatedly."

Feeling an awkward vibe fill the car, Skyler went to turn the radio on once again.

Cane whacked Skyler's hand away one more time. "What did I tell you? Don't touch my stereo. Plus, we are almost there."

Skyler brushed his hair back. "Sorry, just a habit when I think."

Cane cut Skyler off. "You said the wrong thing. Don't worry about it, you were curious. But, I'm a very busy guy. I don't have time for relationships. They're for the young and full of energy like you." Cane turned the car down a side road.

"Well, I'm not in a relationship currently. I'm not really a fan of them." He watched the road unsure where Cane was taking them. "Do you know where you're going?"

"Don't worry, I have been here many times. I know where we're going. But I thought you were with Kax?" Slowing the car down as they got closer.

Shaking his head trying to find any landmarks that weren't thin pine trees. "No, Kax and me aren't together. I liked her. I told her I loved her while on Squall, even proposed to her. But she turned me down and said I didn't have a plan in life and wanted to just be friends. Besides that, I have had like three, maybe four girlfriends in my life. Most of the girls I'm with I don't see more than once."

Cane shook his head laughing. "I'm guessing your mother doesn't know about your appetite, does she?"

Skyler let out a loud chuckle. "I think she might know about the first one, when I was fourteen, but I'm not sure how many more she knows about, or if my uncle told her."

Cane sighed as they pulled up to the spot. "Fourteen? That... young, I wouldn't have guessed. I hope you were safe. I have seen your police record I know you were wild."

Skyler's eyes widened. "What? How do I have a record? I thought they just take you down to the station and call your parents. What's on there? By the way, I'm always safe." Skyler's face was bright red.

"When you applied for the United Galactic Forces, I have to do a background check on all the new cadets. We don't do a basic check; we look at every file possible. Why did you think it was a good idea to use a fake ID at the same location twice?" Cane parked the car undoing his seatbelt.

Skyler got a bit defensive. "I thought maybe different staff wouldn't recognize me, or they would feel sorry for me. I did offer them a bribe. But if I had such a bad record, why did I get accepted?"

Cane grinned like a cat who's about to catch a mouse. "Well your record wasn't bad; no felonies and a few teen misdemeanors for drinking doesn't ruin your record. Plus, even if you were bad, there were ways to get you in. I know you and I wasn't going to let anything stop you from getting in. It's good to know people in high places. Come on now, let's get out of the car. We're here and I want to show you something."

Skyler undid his seatbelt and stepped out of the car. He looked around. The place looked more like the place you would take a date; it was at the top of the hill above the city. No one else was around for miles, there were only trees.

Cane was higher on the hill. He looked back at Skyler. "Come here I want you to see this."

Walking a few feet up the hill. Looking around the place wondering what the reason would be for Cane to take him to a place like this. When he got to the top the answers were clear. "Wow, this is amazing!" Looking down from the top of the hill he could see the lights of the entire city shine like stars in the night sky. Looking up he had an amazingly clear view. Not a view you find many places anymore, with all the Earth light pollution.

Cane put his hand on Skyler's shoulder. "It is one of the best spots I have ever seen. Your dad and I use to come here all the time; sometimes we brought dates, other times it was to watch the world and time go by. Whenever I miss him, I like to come here. I might have traveled the galaxies, but this is still one of my most favorite places."

Skyler watched the stars in amazement. "I used to sleep in the attic at my mom's house. I had a room on the second floor but in the attic, there was a bay window and I would put a cot in there add some pillows and a blanket and just sleep under the stars sometimes."

A gentle tear rolled down Cane's cheek. "There are times you remind me so much of your father. He loved the stars and would do anything to be near them."

"I don't know what to do about my mother. She says she loves me, but she wants to keep me locked away from everything I love."

"Tell her that. Normally if a parent with a higher rank has a concern about their child's line of work, I'm to investigate and potentially relieve them of duty. But I know your situation and no

16

matter what she says you will always have a place in the forces. So, I think you should talk to her."

"I have told you before I haven't talked to her in years, not since I was sixteen. I'm twenty now. I don't know what to say."

Cane turned Skyler to face him and stared at him. "Listen to me, it might be hard but the longer you wait the harder it will be. I will be by your side when you talk to her, if you want. She doesn't like me that much either right now, but I'm willing to try. What's happened between you two anyway?"

Skyler looked away not wanting to think about the past. "Well you know she kept me away from space my entire life. But why I left home? Well, I was kicked out when I was almost 16. She was away at work doing whatever she does for a few weeks and I never got along with my stepdad, Charles. I have no idea why he hates me, but we got into a bad fight. He beat me and threatened to shoot me if I didn't leave. I had nowhere to go so I used my girlfriends' phone and called my Uncle Justin. He came and picked me up and said I could stay with him. I tried to call my mom a few times and Charles always said she was not around and wouldn't let me talk to her. My uncle worked out a time with him to pick up my stuff. My uncle was never home much to begin with, so I pretty much had free reign of his mansion. When I finished school, I told him I was joining UGF and I took as much of my stuff as I could with me, I still have a few things there I will pick up one day. Do I still have my room back at the academy?"

"I'm so sorry I feel like I failed you." Horrified by Skyler's story he began to cry. "Yes, yours and Michael's room are still available. I kept them locked while you were away, knowing you two might not have time to apply for new rooms when you got back. Kax's stuff is stored in your room too because of her roommate." Cane paused. He was struggling with his emotions. "I'm sorry I just can't past what charles did to you. That bastard hit you! I never liked him and if you would have told me I would have been all over him. I remember when you moved out. I hadn't seen you since you were twelve and your mother told me to stay away, but you were turning sixteen and that was special, so I bought you a gift and took it to your house. Charles told me you were at your uncle's and gave me the address. I wanted to see you, but I don't think you were home, so I just dropped the gift off." He gave Skyler a strong hug. "I wish I could have been there for you all these years. Damnit why wasn't I there?"

Skyler's eyes lit up catching a flash of starlight in them. "The model Starship in a bottle, Ya, I got it. It's still packed, as I didn't want to damage it. I didn't know it was you who dropped it off, my uncle just said a friend of my father. I love it and it is a very treasured item." He gave Cane a tight hug.

Not breaking the hug. "You probably don't know this, but that ship was the first gift your father gave me. Your dad was two years younger than me and a higher rank. I was so mad when I became his first officer because I wanted my own ship. He knew this and found ways to torment me about it. Finally, one day I got fed up and was going to quit. Your dad came in with this box and said to me 'I can't give you your own command but here's your own ship.' Right then and there I knew your father was the finest captain I was ever going to meet."

Tears rolled down Skyler's face as he hugged Cane tighter. "I want to go home. This night is just too much."

Cane let go of Skyler and wiped the tears off his cheeks. "Come on, I will drive. You have been through enough trauma tonight you need to relax."

Chapter 3

"What do you mean I don't have a room? I'm a fourth-year cadet you should have a room for me!" Kax yelled at the grey uniformed admissions officer.

The middle-aged dark-haired officer looked at Kax in the eyes and said. "You were not registered as an active on Earth, when the room assignments were decided, Cadet. Normally we would give you another room, but it seems like we are all out of the female dorms."

Her blood boiling and her sharp teeth showing. "Then give me one of the male dorms.

I don't know why there was a mix up in my paperwork. So just give me a room!"

The man typed a few things into the computer. "The only room left in the entire academy is one married dorm, but you have to be married to get it. Are you married?"

Kax thought. She did really need a place. She had the cabin but that is so far away, and she would need a ride. "No, I'm not married but if I have a friend who could share the room with me would that be ok? Does common law count?"

The man typed in a few more things into his computer, rolling his eyes at Kax. "No, Sorry. That's not how marriage works. Common Law works if you wanted an officer's quarters because you can have a max of two people in there. The married ones have two rooms for potential family members. I'm sorry Cadet Tillion, but there are no rooms, you will have to find lodging outside of base for now."

Kax took a deep breath holding back the urge to scratch the man's eyes out and headed to Skyler's room. She knocked on the door, hoping it was still Skyler and Michael's room.

A blond-haired young man wearing only his boxers answered the door brushing his hair back. He looked up at Kax and smiled. "I was wondering when I was going to see you again. Give me a hug you sweet thing."

Rolling her eyes, she pushed Skyler out of the way and entered the room. She could tell Michael had already gone out for breakfast. She noticed that there were boxes of her things in the room stacked at the end of Skyler's bed. Frustrated, she turned to Skyler. "I want to get married!"

His jaw dropped, and his eyes popped out. He cleaned his ear with his figure. "Did I hear you right? You want to get married, is that to me?"

Kax sat on Michael's bed and let out a deep sigh. "I don't have a room. I must find lodging somewhere else off base. The only room left is one married dorm and I can't just have a friend stay with me. I need to be married to get it. Since you always ask me, I figured you would be the most open to marrying me just for me to have my own room."

Skyler sat on his bed and rubbed his forehead. "So, you don't want me, you want a piece of paper with my name on it. Kax if it was any other reason, I would say yes but it is not, this is a dumb reason. If you want a room talk to Cane and don't you already have a house?"

Kax sighed and thought it over. "I do have a place, but I don't have a ride. Plus, my dad is planning on selling it. I'm stuck."

He yawned laying back on his bed. "I have some extra money I could buy you a car if you want. If not, you could always live in this dorm my bed is big enough for two?"

Kax sighed. "I couldn't ask you to buy me a car it wouldn't be fair. And I'm not sharing a bed with you."

Skyler chuckled. "A minute ago, you wanted to marry me, now you don't want to have anything to do with me. You women are so hard to understand."

"I wanted to marry you not sleep with you! And what are my boxes doing in your room. I hope you didn't look through them!"

Rolling onto his side to look at the boxes while laughing. "Let's get one thing straight. If I ever get married, I will want sex, I will not live in a sexless marriage. That's not for me. So, if you were serious about marrying me for this little piece of paper so you could have a room, sex would be expected. Marriage is a serious commitment I don't throw around lightly. And I didn't touch your stuff the tape is still on the boxes. Cane had your stuff stored here because my room was locked up because me and Michael were both gone, but your roommate was still using your room."

Kax crossed her legs and sighed. "As long as you didn't touch my stuff, were good."

Skyler sat up on the bed. "Kax, I got in real late last night, all I did was go to bed. Your stuff is fine. I care about you and respect your privacy, I'm not going to touch anything without your permission."

Kax got up off the bed and went over to check the cardboard boxes of all her stuff. She opened the top box to see what was inside.

Skyler leaned over to watch her as she rummaged through her stuff. "What kind of things do you have in there anyway?"

Leaning over the box to cover the top. Not wanting Skyler to see what was inside. "Don't look at my stuff."

Skyler got off his bed, pulled a box out from under his bed. The box had blue tape on the top. "If you don't want me to look then don't look in your boxes with me around. But to be fair, I will show you what is in this box of mine. What do you really have in their dirty clothes?"

Kax looked in her box. *He's right you know, there are not many personal things in here except for a few pictures. I'm curious to see what he has in his box, though.* "Okay, I will show you what is in my box, but I want to see what's in yours."

Skyler conceded, removing the thin blue masking tape from the top of his box. "I just want you to know that this stuff is really personal to me and I have never shown anyone else these things."

Kax rolled her eyes. "You're not going to show me a box of dirty magazines, are you?"

Ignoring her comment, he took a black and silver picture frame out of the box and passed it to Kax.

Kax looked at the picture inside and saw a young blond-haired man wearing a cadet uniform like their own. With straight blond hair, green eyes and strong facial features, she examined the picture for over a minute. "This is your dad's cadet photo, isn't it?"

Skyler looked down at Kax with half a smile. "Ya, it is. When my dad died my mom put all this stuff away. One night I found the stuff and took some things out of there. Keeping them hidden from her. Knowing if she knew I had them she would take them away."

Kax handed him the photo back. "You look so much like your father in that picture."

A humble smiled came across his face. He pulled out another item from the box. This time, it was a plush spaceship. It was green and oval shaped, with brown spots and looked like it had been chewed on. "Before you say anything this was my baby toy. My mom told me my dad bought it for me on my first birthday. It's old and needs a good washing, but it was my first ship."

She held it in her hand for a moment examining it. Then looking back up at Skyler. "It's adorable and precious."

Skyler took it back. "Ya, and I know I have never washed it because I'm worried about damaging it."

Before Skyler can pull out another item out of the box Kax reached into her box and searched for an item. "You have shown me two things it's my turn to show you at least one."

She handed Skyler a dark blue metal picture frame.

Skyler took the frame and looked at the picture. There were two girls in the picture. One, an older woman with red hair and pink cat ears with a fluffy tail and the other, a little girl about five with strawberry blond hair and a big smile on her face holding a little cat doll. He looked at the picture for a minute, examine the similarities of the mother and daughter and smiled. "Your mom is very beautiful and that's a cute cat doll you have there."

Embarrassed, Kax grabbed the picture back. "Stop it. You're trying to tease me, aren't you?"

The smile faded. "No, I was giving you a compliment, I think it is a great picture of you and your mom. You look so happy together. You now look a lot like your mom. Also, you were a cute kid, who liked cats."

She put the picture back in the box where he couldn't see it. "I don't mind cats, but I only had that doll because it was the only doll my dad could find me on Earth that had ears like me."

The door to the room opened and Michael walked in with a takeout container of food. He looked around and saw Kax and Skyler with the open boxes sitting on the floor. "You guys moving in together or something?"

Skyler put his stuff back into the box. "No, we're just sharing old memories. Where did you go to get a takeout container?"

Michael handed Skyler the takeout container. "The cafeteria now has them. I am not sure why, but I brought you some breakfast since you like to skip it."

Skyler opened the styrofoam container. Inside was some fruit and replicated hash browns. "Michael, I told you I don't like breakfast when I have been drinking."

Michael rolled his eyes. "Fruit is good for you and I know you love replicated hash browns."

Skyler examined the food and took a bite out of one of the hash browns. "Oh, boy, have I missed these, the cafeteria always knows how to make them better than all the other replicators."

Michael grabbed a piece of melon out of Skyler's takeout tray. He sat down on his bed chewing the piece. "Well, Skyler you will soon have a new roommate."

Skyler frowned finishing off his hash brown and offered Kax the other one and she just took a piece of melon. "What's wrong Michael, you're not dropping out, are you?"

Michael pulled a piece of paper out of his pocket. "I just went by the office to get my schedule for classes and I don't have any. Because, remember last year, when I created the new alloy? Well, I am now entering my fifth year, they are putting me on work duty. They said I could keep my room, but I will have a random work schedule. It will be like that until I get a posting. I have put in a request for officer's quarters."

Kax perked up and smiled. "Michael if you get one want to move in together and be common law?"

Skyler rolled his eyes. "Ugh, not this again."

Michael's eyes popped. "Uh, do you mean to you?"

Skyler cut in. "She asked me earlier. She needs a room and the only one free is a married dorm and so she wants to marry one of us to get it. I said yes but she doesn't want to sleep with me."

"He's paraphrasing." Kax hissed at Skyler.

Michael laughed and brushed his hair back. "No, I do not want to get married but that's for personal reasons. I thought you had the cabin nearby you could stay at."

Skyler answered for Kax again. "She does but no ride." He thought for a minute. "Hey, Michael has a ride and he needs a place, so why don't all three of us move into your cabin. You said no one is using it, we could move in and I could get a car."

Getting annoyed with Skyler always cutting in she did listen to his idea. "It's not what I would have planned. But remember my dad is selling the house and might not be happy with me living with two guys, but I could ask."

Michael thought about it. "If it is going to bother your father, we do not have to do this."

Skyler piped in. "Just give me ten minutes on the phone with your dad and we will be set. Parents love me."

Kax and Michael looked at each other rolling their eyes.

"Skyler please don't talk to my dad I have a feeling that girls' fathers really don't like you that much." She gets off the floor and pulls out her commentator out of her pocket, calling her dad's number. "One-minute guys."

"Hello, David Tillion speaking." Said the voice on the other line.

"Hi, daddy, it's me. I don't have much time, but I have a question to ask you."

"Sure, sweetie, anything you want."

"There was a shortage of rooms this year and so I need a place to say. Skyler is getting a car and Michael needs a place to stay as well. So, I was wondering if we could all stay in the cabin for the school year." Her voice sounding extra sweet and fast as she talked.

"As long as you all have separate rooms, I guess. I was going to get the place ready to sell next weekend, but I guess if your friends are going to be staying there you could all pay rent?"

A look of hurt fell over Kax's face. "Daddy you would charge your own daughter rent?"

"Why do you think I'm selling the place? I can't afford the bills on it. It's massive."

Skyler grabbed the communicator from Kax and said to her father. "Hello Mr. Tillion, this is Skyler Therris, Kax's good-looking friend, we met yesterday. I will have no problem paying the bills for that lovely cabin. Kax loves that place and it would break her heart to lose it and I have no intention of ever seeing that happen. And to help you out I won't just pay the bills. I will get my uncle to buy the place from you? How does that sound? You have probably heard of my uncle, Justin Munroe? And Kax can come and visit it as much as she likes now, how does that sound?"

The room was silent. Kax and Michael looked at each other in shock of what they just heard. Both were worried to hear what David would say. They watched Skyler in awe.

After a moment Skyler handed the phone back to Kax. "He wants to speak to you."

Kax took the phone. "Hello, Daddy."

David took a deep breath and after a minute responded with. "I don't know what that boy's intentions with you are, but please be safe. I have tried to keep that house in the family for the past 20 years, but it is very expensive but if what he is saying is true then I'm going to agree to it."

Kax smiled. "Don't worry Michael and Skyler are safe. Michael knows how to keep Skyler down. I'm certain Skyler's uncle will come through. We will be in touch ok daddy?"

"Okay, sweetie. Enjoy your cabin."

She turned off the phone. She and Michael just stared at Skyler. "Thank you, Skyler, for being my hero again."

"No problem." Skyler looked across the room at Michael, grinning. "I guess we are going car shopping."

Chapter 4

Michael sat alone in Fleet Admiral Cane's office. He was waiting for the admiral to arrive; the secretary had told him to wait in the office.

"Sorry to keep you waiting, Michael. It's the beginning of the year and lots of things are going on. I just got back from orientation." Cane was wearing his gold satin dress uniform. "So, Michael how was your summer?"

"My summer was fine. I stated almost every detail in my report about it." Michael answered. "But I really want to know what is being done with the worm orb now that it is in Earth's hands?"

"I read your report. It was very detailed and I'm glad we don't print them out no more. It would have been a novel thick. But it was a secret mission, so I had to delete it from my records. Remember for next time; secret missions don't get reports. As for the orb, I have passed it on to the higher-ups and it is up to them to decide what is to be done with it. I can't tell you anymore because I don't know."

"I see, sir." Michael paused to think. "What became of Dr. Haas?"

Cane let out a short chuckle. "Oddly enough I'm not sure. When the security guards went to get him out of the brig he wasn't there. I checked the crew manifest and there was no record of him. The most details we have on him are what was in your report ironically. We have video footage of him and detailed descriptions but how he posed as a member of the United Galactic Forces, we may never know."

**

Monday afternoon, an electric green convertible hover car pulled up to the main entrance to the academy, right to the front doors. Kax was standing in the doorway of the academy. "You skipped school to buy a convertible? I thought you were going to buy something practical."

Skyler brushed his hair back. "You misunderstood, I was going to buy you something practical. But you told me you didn't want me to buy you a car and we still needed a car. I figured why not get something I'd enjoy." He rubbed the black leather passenger seat. "You can enjoy it too."

She walked around the car examining its features. It had all black interior. Decent sized back seat. But a small trunk. She fingered the car as she walked around it. "Well it is your money, but how are we supposed to pack our boxes into this?"

He turned his head to look at her. "That's what the back seat is for and there is some trunk space. We will figure it out. Now do you want to get into the car and go for a ride?"

I'm going to regret this. She hopped into the passenger's side.

Skyler put one hand on the wheel and one arm around her and stepped on the gas. He sped out of campus and headed for the highway. Going way faster than anyone should.

"Hey isn't that Michael?" Kax pointed ahead. Hoping Skyler would slow the car down.

He honked and pulled over.

Michael pulled up beside Skyler. "I waited for you, I thought you were going to get a ride back with me to the cabin?"

Grinning, all proud he said, "I changed my mind. I Skipped class and got a car instead. I got a ride into the city with Miri."

28

Michael groaned. "Please tell me next time. I know we have the thirty-minute rule but if you can send me a message. I am heading back to the cabin for some rest. I got to help with a project tonight. Enjoy the car and slow down your going to get a speeding ticket."

Skyler scoffed. "A ticket doesn't bother me. I'll try to message you next time. I'm just going to take Kax someplace and then head back to class." His right-hand moved down towards her breast.

She twisted his hand and snapped. "Touch me again there and I will break more than your hand! Let's just go back to the dorm now."

Wincing in pain Skyler took his arm away from Kax. "Sorry Kax, I was only joking. I would only do that if you wanted me to, but I will keep my hands off."

"Let's just get back to the dorm," Kax hissed back.

"I really did want to take you somewhere that wasn't a joke." He said turning the car around.

"Another time," she replied.

Michael waved goodbye and they all continued their journey.

Chapter 5

"And that is the last box," Michael said as he got the boxes packed into the convertible.

"But now I can't go fast on the road, the car is weighed down too much," Skyler whined as he looked at his new car filled with boxes.

"Well we could leave that box with the blue tape on it behind. It felt like the heaviest of them all." Michael snarkily replied.

Skyler glared. "You touch those boxes and I will make you regret ever being born."

Michael smugly smiled. "Good now, Skyler head up to the cabin at the speed limit and me and Kax will follow behind you on the bike."

Skyler looked back at the dorms. He looked down the white grey halls he had called home for the last two years. He wondered if he was going to ever live in those dorms again. Taking a moment to remember the past. He stood there outside of the corridor doors saying goodbye to his memories. He walked to the car and was about to step in when he saw Cane walking up the path.

Out of breath from rushing to catch them, Cane said. "Where do you three think you are going? I heard from the admissions officer you've given up the dorm?"

Kax nodded. "Yes, they told me that there weren't any rooms left and Michael has a mixed-up schedule, so we all decided to just move to my- I mean Skyler's cabin."

Cane raised an eyebrow and mumbled, "So the cabin has reverted to Skyler." Cane noticed Skyler's new car while Kax was talking. He responded to Kax. "If you would have talked to me, I would have found you a room. But if you kids want to try this go ahead but remember you're all on call."

Skyler walked around the car back towards Cane and next to Kax. "We will be fine. Michael has a bike, so we will be able to travel back and forth at different times. Like my new car?"

Cane nodded his head. "It's nice, green seems to be your color."

Skyler smirked. "Hey what can I say, it's a chick magnet that matches my eyes."

Cane patted Skyler on the shoulder then walked over to Michael and handed him a piece of paper. He whispered into Michael's ear, "See me in my office tomorrow before class." He waved goodbye to them. "You kids have a safe trip and I expect to see you all in class on time tomorrow."

They all waved to Cane as he walked away, got into their vehicles and drove off.

Chapter 6

Morning arrived and with all the unpacking of the night before Michael almost forgot about his meeting with Cane. He was reminded when his tablet pinged sending him a reminder of the appointment. He sat up in his bed and checked the time on the clock. *Going to be late got to get going.* He jumped out of bed and began to get dressed. *I wonder what Cane needs to see me about so badly? Maybe it has to do with my odd course schedule?* His schedule didn't make much sense to him. Most engineering cadets are made to graduate at year four because they just need to know their skill level unless they're in a special division. He was now a working while still a cadet. *Cane must know something and that's why he kept me off the frontlines.* That was the only thing he could think of. Because if he would have taken the early graduation he wouldn't be worrying where he rested his head at night, if he still had a head to rest.

He got dressed and headed down to the kitchen. He looked in the fridge and remembered they were out of food. Last night they had ordered a pizza and Skyler had eaten all the leftovers. The only thing left was the box of fish sticks, in the freezer. He groaned at the irony. *Nothing in the fridge,* he was not going to eat the fish sticks. *Guess I am going to class without breakfast,* he thought. He left a note saying he had to talk to Cane before class and left early. He grabbed his jacket and made his way back to the base.

At the Academy Michael double checked his timetable for the area he was supposed to go to for his new classes. He was going to an area he had never been to. He was glad his new schedule came with directions; if not he would be lost. Heading down the halls of the academy he noticed was going to pass by Cane's office. He was starting to wonder what kind of class he was going to if it was so close to the Fleet Admiral's office and not in the engineering building. Before going to class, he figured he would check and see if Cane was in his office.

He walked through the gray steel door. It was so early in the morning the secretary was not even in the office. The door was unlocked so someone had to be there. He kept going to the back where the door to Cane's office was. He looked in through the glass window and saw an exhausted-looking Cane. He lightly knocked on the door.

Cane picked up his head and waved Michael in.

Michael opened the door to the office. "Morning Cane, you wanted to see me?"

Cane reached over his desk and poured a glass of brandy for himself. "Do you want a glass?"

Shaking his head, Michael sat down at the desk. "I do not drink this early in the morning."

Cane took a big sip of his drink. "It's not morning when you haven't been able to sleep for two days. If I had it my way you kids would have stayed on Squall longer."

Michael's eyes narrow. "Why? What would be the purpose of that?"

"To keep you kids safe." Cane yawned. "I knew I could get you to get the orb for us. I also knew I needed a good team. I'm not sure what it is but you three get along so good together. But sending someone to do command training on Squall is just a credited vacation. You were all chosen for a reason to go. And if I could I would have kept you there this year. We have received warnings from the Cass they are planning more attacks. Earth is not going to be a safe place. All three of you among many others on this base have such potential to do much more." Cane took a sip of his drink. "That's what I hate most about war. So many brilliant innocent young people get killed before they get the chance to show it."

Michael's hand trembled in worry. "Sir, is that why I am a working cadet this year and not graduating?"

"Short answer, yes." Cane finished his drink. "With the restrictions I was supposed to have you graduate when you returned to earth, but with your ideas and inventions, myself and admiral Ipinik felt graduation was not right for you right now. I was able to hold you back for more training, it's not a standard program that's why you have such a strange schedule."

"You mean standard for a Squallite?" Michael scoffed. "Because almost every division has a seven-year program as well."

Cane sighed, "That's one way of looking at it and there are Squallite's in the seven-year programs. Your forces career is not why I called you here to talk. There are other important things to discuss. Such as there is going to be an attack on the base tomorrow. After a bomb is going to go off. We have people searching for the the bombs now and security is upped but we are not sure if it has been planted yet." Cane pulled a briefcase out from under his desk. He placed the case on the desk facing Michael and opened it, revealing three laser guns. "I want you to take this case and arm yourself. I know I wrote out a plan for tomorrow, but they may not strike when told. I also know these are only to be used by high ranking security officers. But if anyone stops you tell them to check the serial numbers. I have gotten a special release for you three and a few others to have them. There are a few others with them around base. Don't worry about wearing them around base."

Michael leaned forward reaching for one of the guns. Picking it up he examined it. They had one barrel with a power converter. They were about nine inches long. He was left in awe over the sight of them. "So, we do one mission for you now you want us to do more?"

Cane sighed, "It's not like that. There is something special about you kids and you always seem to jump at the opportunities to be a heroes. You can always say no."

Michael examined the gun in his hand. *Things have improved for me since Skyler came into my life. Also keeping up with these missions has been working in my favor as well.* "I'll do it and pass the message on."

Cane smiled, "There are holsters in the zipped compartment at the top. You can wear them any way you like. I said before they're registered for you so don't worry about them being exposed or not."

Michael put the gun back into the case and closed it. "I will make sure Kax and Skyler get theirs. I have no idea what you have planned for us in the future but, thank you."

Cane filled his glass again. "Do not put those guns on low, I want them locked on high. When the attack starts, and you see a Cassiopaean, shoot and do not hesitate; we have no idea what to expect from them this time."

Michael took the briefcase off the table. "I do not know what is going on here, but I will follow these orders."

Cane rubbed his forehead and leaned back in his chair. "In some ways, I'm glad you kids moved off base. I hope you enjoy that cabin. Don't get me wrong Michael, I care about you kids, I care about all of my cadets, but I try to do everything in my power for your best interest."

Michael looked at the window on the wall behind Cane's chair. He saw the sun rising, the day getting closer. "Sir, I would love to stay and talk more, but I need to get to class. Please get some sleep."

Cane laughed waving Michael out. "Get going, you're going to need all the hours you can. I will sleep when I know everything is safe."

Michael gave Cane a worried smile. "Well do not worry, we will be fine." As Michael walked out of the office with the briefcase in hand, he had a grim feeling fall over him. This whole mission seemed wrong. He was an engineer, not a warrior. He knew this had to be done and just how many more cadets were doing this mission.

He didn't like guns and it made him feel queasy that he was caring a case of them. Guns that he knew that would take lives.

He walked to his new classroom, unsure what to expect. He saw a blue door with a big red 96 painted on the top. That was his class. He placed his hand on the round metal doorknob but it was locked. He jerked the lock, thinking the door was just jammed. He put the briefcase down and pulled his tablet out of his pocket and looked at the schedule again. All it said was 'Classroom 96, then go to the second floor in the main building and go down the hall till you see a blue door with a red 96 then enter.' Confused and worried now he hoped he wasn't too early. Unsure what he should do he stood in front of the door, waiting for something to happen.

A skinny maroon-haired Cadet with brown eyes, wearing a green uniform came down the hall. He saw Michael. "Hello, you must be Michael Jones, my name is Rob Thorne. I'll show you how to open the door." He walked in front of the door and put his hand on the left side opposite of the knob. The door pushed open. Rob looked back at Michael. "It's a trick door. They don't want anyone just walking in here."

Michael entered the room with Rob. "But how does it lock?"

Rob turned on the light switch on in the inside of the doorway. "It locks from the inside as there is another entrance that only the commodore knows of and he has a camera and knows when students are showing up for class and unlocks it."

Michael stared around the now illuminated classroom. It looked like a science lab with all the beakers and microscopes on the counters next to the round counter-like desks. In the back of the room he could see a row of computers. There were model ships hanging from the ceiling. While looking around the room. He said, "What kind of classroom is this?"

Rob smiled and sat down at one of the curved desks. "Advanced engineering. It goes beyond what you know as an engineer. It takes some old some new and creates a whole new thing."

Michael sat down next to Rob placing the briefcase between his legs. "If this is engineering why are you wearing a command uniform?"

Rob grinned. "Like I said, it's advanced engineering, that means cadets who have shown they know something a little more about engineering than everyone else. I'm still in the command division but engineering is my second."

Michael shifted his eyes around the room once again. "Why are we the only ones here? Are we early?"

"No were on time." Rob looked around the room. "There are some here in the basement." He pointed to the staircase in the back of the room. "There will be more cadets soon."

They both turned in their seats when they heard footsteps coming from the back of the class where the computer was.

The white-haired Squallite Commodore stepped into the room grinning with all his attention on Michael. "Well now you must be Michael, glad you could show up to class."

Michael stood up and held out his hand to the approaching teacher. "Nice to meet you, Commodore, uh…"

He took Michael's hand. "Gray, Commodore Gray. It is nice to meet you too, you're the only new student in this class this year. I'm impressed with your record. What was your inspiration in creating that alloy?"

Michael sighed. "Well Commodore Gray, it was a mixture of a lot of fear and stress."

Gray patted Michael on the back. "Good, at least we know what makes you tick, I'll use that." He pulled out his tablet and tapped the screen three times.

A group of ten Cadets entered the room of all different races and uniforms. They all took their seats around the table facing the front.

Michael sat back down in his seat. His heart still racing with anxiety. He copied the class and stared at the front, where Commodore Gray was standing.

He picked up a light blue binder that was sitting on top of his desk. He opened it somewhere in the middle of all the white pages. "Okay class today I'm going to talk to you a bit about holograms and their importance in combat. You have all morning with me, so this will be interesting."

***

"Skyler could you please slow down the car!" Kax yelled while trying to hold onto something for dear life, as Skyler sped down the road.

Showing no signs of slowing down. "Look Kax, it is a convertible, it's meant to be driven fast. I can't slow down even if I wanted to, it would make the car feel bad."

Glaring at Skyler, "It's a car so it has no feelings and I want to get to school alive. I'm not impressed by fast cars. So slow down and later you can take a few girls out in the new car and drive as fast as you want."

Reaching into his pocket he held out a spare set of keys. "Here Kax, just in case I do get lucky tonight, I want you to drive the car back and I will stay overnight."

Taking the key, "What do you mean get lucky? You sound like you already have this all planned out?"

"I have just thought it through, and I think it is a good idea if you have the spare key. Just I'm the only one who can have dates in the car."

Rolling her eyes. "Trust me I won't have sex in a car ever again."

Skyler slowed down the car to just below the speed limit. "What do you mean again? When did you have sex in my car?"

"Not in your car!" She covered her face. "I don't want to talk about it. It's ancient history, back when I was in high school."

Skyler kept the car at the slow pace. He grinned imagining Kax in the backseat of his own car. "You can trust me I won't tell anyone."

Taking a deep breath, she said. "One of my ex-boyfriend's use to drive me home from school. Before we got home, he would get me to have sex with him or do something sexual. Our relationship didn't last long, and I wish it was shorter since he was a jerk."

"Sounds like it," Skyler put his right hand on Kax's shoulder rubbing it comfortingly. "I'm sorry to hear that. You do know if I was in school with you, I wouldn't have let any man hurt you."

She shifted away from Skyler. "I know we're just friends, so don't use my pain as an excuse to try and hit on me."

He jerked the car and pulled onto the side of the road and shifted to look at Kax. "Listen to me, I do like you, a lot. I do care about you. Yes, I do hit on you a little more than I should, but that's just me. It's sort of my thing, I do it to all women. You have told me that you want to be friends and I'm respectful of that. I'm also the guy who doesn't like to see women hurt or upset. If we knew each other in high school, even if I didn't and I heard that someone wasn't treating a girl right, I would've knocked them out. I'm a guy who likes women. It might seem like I'm just a prick who cares about their bodies, but it's more than that. I find girls who are just looking for some fun nothing else. That's what makes you different Kax, I know you're not that type of girl, but something makes me love you because of that. I believe in respecting women, I don't want to see any women hurt, you got that?"

Kax looked deep into Skyler's eyes. She knew if he had ever told the truth in his life this was it. "I believe you."

He shifted back into a driving position and resumed driving at the speed limit.

Chapter 7

Michael was finished his morning class and was quickly making his way to the cafeteria before the whole food court ran out. He was starving. He had missed breakfast and really could use something real in his stomach after last night's veggie pizza. Holding onto the briefcase, he headed to the door to leave with the other students.

Commodore Gray called to him. "Michael, please come see me."

Michael stopped in his tracks. He turned away from the door and made his way to the Commodore's desk. "Yes, sir?" He wondered what Commodore Gray wanted from him.

Gray waited till the last student had left, "I'm going to guess that something big is going down if you are carrying a case of three H4's and they are locked on high."

Michael froze, his eyes huge and his heart stopped. "How would you know that, sir?"

Gray grinned like the hungry cat who had found his prey. "When you stand at the doorway, I have an x-ray camera on all students. To make sure they are not carrying any weapons or methods to steal other projects. I would've stopped you from coming in here, but I ran the registration code on the guns and found out they're under Fleet Admiral Cane's name and know not to mess with his orders. I know there are rumors of an attack tomorrow and I know H4's are almost never given to students. So, what do you know?"

Frozen like a statue, feeling like a child who had been caught by their mother for stealing a cookie out of the cookie jar before supper. He took a deep breath. "I don't know, but me and my friends are supposed to shoot to kill any Cassiopean we see tomorrow after the attack has started. Also, there might be a bomb."

"A bomb you say?" Gray smirked. "You may go now thank you for telling me this information. Be sure to let Commodore Roch know. He's your afternoon teacher."

"Yes, Sir." Michael nodded and headed out of the room with the case. Once out of the class he rushed down to the cafeteria. When he got there, he jumped in line hoping there was at least a fruit cup left. In the line, he looked and saw the last fruit cup. He was too far to reach it. He tried to get it when a brunette Catillion grabbed it. Frustrated, he moved the Sagittarian in front of him out of the way and squeezing his way ahead in line he tapped the Catillion on the shoulder. "Excuse me, I wanted that fruit cup."

She turned to look at him with her green cat eyes. "I got it first, so it's mine."

He glared at the short cat-like girl in front of him. "I'm a Squallite so I can only eat whole food, nothing replicated. I missed breakfast and that's the last bit of whole food left for sale so please give me the fruit cup."

She put on her charm. "Learn to eat replicated, this fruit cup is mine."

A hand touched Michael's shoulder. Kax was reaching over from outside the line. "Let her have the fruit cup, I already got you your lunch."

Michael stopped arguing and looked over at Kax. He saw a fruit cup and granola in her hand. He tried to wiggle out of the line. He ignored the rude Catillion and went with his friend.

Kax led him to their table.

Skyler had already started eating his replicated pasta salad.

Kax sat down and moved the extra tray over to Michael's side. She put the fruit cup and granola next to a garden salad on his tray.

Michael sat down next to Kax. He placed the briefcase on the table next to him. He opened the container for his salad and started to eat it with his fork in hand. The tasteless lettuce tasted sweeter than normal in his hungry mouth.

Skyler was staring at the silver briefcase on the table. He put down his fork. "What's in the case?"

Michael finished his bite of food. "Three H4's one for each of us. Registered to Fleet Admiral Cane."

Kax's heart stopped and her eyes widen. "Is this because of your meeting this morning?"

Michael nodded. "Cane gave them to me this morning. All day tomorrow we are needed to wear these. They are locked on high and we are to shoot any Cass we see once the attack starts."

Skyler frowned. "What about the Cass that are students, we don't shoot them right?"

This whole conversation bothered Michael. He hated guns and didn't like violence or people getting hurt. *But this is a time of war,* he kept telling himself. "No, do not shoot Cadets unless it is obvious, they are part of the attack. No one knows what time tomorrow the attack is and only a few know about it."

Skyler leaned over grabbing the case. He popped the locks open and looked inside the case. "Wow, those are lovely."

Michael tried to close the case, but Skyler's hand was in the way. "We are in a public place so I do not think we should be flashing these around."

Skyler smirked. "You said Cane gave them to us. What if the Cass don't attack tomorrow and they decide to come early? We are best to be armed now. The red security cadets wear their guns all the time why not us?"

Kax cut in. "He does have a point you know. I don't like this gun idea either, but you did say we are not to fire them until the attack starts so I don't see them causing any harm."

Michael didn't even want to hold these guns let alone use them. But his friends did have a point. He lifted the case. "There are holsters in the zipper." He went back to eating his food.

Skyler unzipped the top and pulled out the holsters. He held one up. They were black and adjustable. They converted so you can either wear them on your waist or shoulders. He took one and handed it to Kax and put Michael's near him. Taking his and placing it over his shoulder's. He took one of the guns out of the case out of the inlay foam. Looking over the blue steel nine-inch gun. Holding it in one hand and rubbed it with the other. Examining the energy converter on the front around the barrel. He had a smile of a child receiving a new toy.

Kax rolled her eyes. "Put the gun away, it's not a toy." She stood up putting her holster around her hip and around her right leg on the right side where the slit in her skirt was. She took the gun and placed it in the holster. She sat down and went back to her food.

Michael who was eating his food the entire time looked at the last gun in the case. He didn't want to leave the gun exposed or carry it around in the case anymore. It was a busy cafeteria everyone could've seen what is in the case now. He got up and put the holster around his waist and placed in the gun. "Skyler do you want to take the case to your car? I do not want to lose it, but I don't want to carry it around all day."

Skyler put his gun in his holster and closed the case. "Sure, I have no problem doing that."

They worked on finishing their lunches when the Catillion from the lineup came by the table. "Hi there, sir, I wanted to apologize for being rude in the lineup."

Michael looked at her and shook his head. "I was the rude one. I was making you give up your food that you had gotten fair and square."

She sat down next to Skyler. "Yes, but I eat replicated food and you have a special dietary plan. Normally, I would have let you have the cup, but it was mostly melon." She put her hand on Skyler's thigh.

"It is fine I will not die if I eat some replicated food, good thing my friend here got me my lunch for me." Michael raised an eyebrow at Skyler.

Skyler cut in. "You know melon is also my favorite fruit."

She turned her attention to Skyler. "Really, I'm glad to hear that. My favorite is Honey Dew."

Skyler shifted closer to her. "I'm going to guess you love honeydew melon so much you have one in your dorm room?"

She whispered into his ear. "Why don't you come with me and find out."

Skyler and the girl got out of the seat. "Hey, Kax will you put the case in the car for me when you are done with lunch?"

Kax groaned. "Yes, and I will put your lunch tray away. Just hand me your gun and keys."

Without question, he took the H4 out of its holster and handed it over to Kax. Then he pulled his set of keys out of his pocket and placed them on the table.

The girl had her hands all over his torso. "Why does he need to give you his gun?"

Kax reached up and took the gun. "Because I doubt you will need it in the next thirty minutes, and we don't need it to go off before he does."

The girl shot Kax an annoyed look.

Skyler kissed the girl on her neck and waved to Kax and Michael as he walked away with the girl.

Michael scratched his head. "Did I miss something?"

Kax laughed putting the gun back in its case. "She came over here to pick up Skyler. Probably because of his weapon. Since she saw you, she used the fruit cup story as an excuse."

"I knew these guns were a bad idea." Michael finished his last bite of food and got up. "Well then I guess we better get going, he is gone, and we've got things to do."

Once in the nameless female Catillion's dorm, Skyler didn't waste time taking off his clothes. He kissed her onto the bed, helping her with her clothes. Lifted her skirt and rolled down her leggings, carefully taking them off.

She unzipped her top and unhooking her bra from the front said. "Come up here and play with my melons." She spoke suggestively.

Skyler kissed her body all the way up. He rubbed her breasts.

She kissed his neck.

He got his pelvis into position and caressed her hips.

She began to purr at the feeling of his touch.

He stopped unsure of the sound he was hearing. "What is that?"

She giggled. "You mean my purring? Catillion's do that when they are enjoying something. It's our equivalent to your moaning."

His eyes lit up. "Right, forgot about that. It's kind of hot, I noticed how your chest vibrated too. I have never been with a Catillion before, so I don't know much about their bodies."

She purred a bit more pulling him on top of her. "Well I will tell you this, our orgasms last longer, and we love our butts and hips played with."

He rubbed her hips listening to her purr. "Nice, just like a real cat. Could you teach me a few more tricks I want to get better with you Catillions…"

She kissed him to silence him. "Play with my ears and hurry it along. Also, don't think about that other girl while we do this. But I think we can both benefit each other."

Playing with her black ears, he heard her purr more and more. He rubbed her body and thrust his hips. She wasn't Kax, but she was someone in between. He knew he was going to learn a lot from this girl.

Chapter 8

"Skyler are you ready?" Kax hollered up the stairs towards Skyler's room.

Skyler came down the stairs still doing up his pants. "I can't believe you are this excited to die."

Kax rolled her eyes. "We're not going to die and what took you so long to get dressed? You have been up there for half an hour."

Walking right next to Kax and putting his arm around her and walking with her to the kitchen. "Well let's just say I needed a clear head before I went into battle."

A disgusted look came over her face. Quickly she jerked away from Skyler. "Don't do that again."

He busted out laughing. "And you didn't? This might be our last chance for fun what else was I supposed to do?"

Covering her face. "We're not going to die so don't think of it as your last day."

Skyler sighed and went to the kitchen looking in the fridge for a quick snack. "Why is there only health food in the fridge?" He pulled his head out of the fridge and looked at Kax who was now standing beside him. "Why did Michael buy food for him and not us yesterday?"

Kax grabbed an apple off the counter and handed it to Skyler. "Because he went shopping and you told him you would do your own later, which we haven't done yet. So, have an apple they're good for you."

Skyler turned around taking the apple. "Well, I guess I have no choice. If we live through this attack, we will party and buy groceries."

"We're going to live."

***

Michael watched the clock. His mind was too distracted. He couldn't do any work in class as his mind was worried about the impending cloud of doom that was to befall all of them.

Commodore Gray walked up behind Michael's chair. "Go for a walk, you're dismissed from class."

Michael jerked around in his chair closing his textbook. "Sir, why should I skip class if I am working?"

Gray placed his hand on Michael's shoulder. "Because you're not working, now get out of class before your head explodes."

Michael packed his bags and walking out of the classroom. Keeping his nervous hand on his gun.

Rob Thorn was walking down the hall returning to class, "Hey!" He called out to him.

Michael nervous and jumpy drew his gun and pointed it at Rob.

Rob stopped and raised his hands. "Hey, watch it, dude, I was just trying to be friendly."

Michael put the gun back and looked at Rob. "Sorry, I need to do something please go back to class. I'm a little on edge."

Rob looked Michael over. "I have killed before if you need any help with your mission."

Eyes widened. "No, I don't and I'm not out to kill anyone please leave me alone."

Rob didn't move. "I know you are up to something and I'm going to stay right by your side."

Michael sighed knowing this guy had no plans to leave him. "Well then what do you know about defusing a bomb?"

Rob's face lit up like a forest fire. "More than any sane man should know."

"Okay, then come with me I have to see if I can find it. No idea where it is just that there might be one somewhere in the academy." Michael rushed through the deserted hall.

Rob quickly behind him. "Wait, so there's a real bomb in the academy?"

Rushing trying to see if he could hear or smell something odd. "Yes, there is. It is believed there will be an attack on Academy today. I am supposed to find a bomb and shoot any enemy Cassiopaean's that I see."

Trying to keep up. "How will you know they're enemies and not cadets?"

"People keep asking me that question, I am guessing for one they will not be wearing a cadet uniform." Michael's worry and stress levels grew. He hoped he would not hurt anyone innocent.

**

Skyler tapped his pencil on his desk while his other hand shook. He looked out the window next to his desk. He could see the main hangar from here. He knew he should go out and be searching for the bomb, but he was so worried about the dangers of this attack he just sat in class and waited for that red alert light to go off. He didn't want to die. He didn't want the school to be attacked, but he didn't want to wait for the enviable. He knew what was coming. He just wanted to get it over with already.

O'Brien had finished talking and was now sitting down at their desk. Skyler was so distracted he didn't hear a word they were saying. Was he supposed to open his book to a certain page or were they just going to study? He leaned over to see if he could tell what the other students were doing, but it seemed like they all were doing something different. No two classmates were on the same page or even looking in the same book. If this was a study class what were they studying?

Worried and frustrated he got up out of his seat. He didn't care anymore about the class. he had to go and see Kax. *She is probably just as frustrated as me,* he thought. He walked out of the class not caring if O'Brien even noticed. Quickly walking down, the halls, he stopped. He noticed a man who was going into the janitor closet who was clearly not a staff member. Only seeing the back of him he slowly moved closer. The man in the non-issued blue coveralls went into the closet closing the door behind him. Skyler drew his weapon and rushed to the door. He looked in through the small glass window. It's clear now who and what this man was. He was a Cassiopaean and he was planting a Bomb.

Skyler guarded the door, holding his gun in one hand he pulled his communicator out with his other and called Michael.

"Hello, Cadet Jones, speaking."

Skyler tried to speak calmly. "Michael, I'm in building A and there is a Cass in the janitor closet who is planting a bomb. I'm watching the door. I'm on the first floor between rooms 120 and 124."

"I am diffusing a bomb! How many are there?" Michael took a deep breath. "Okay Skyler, I am sending someone to help you with the bomb. Rob said not to shoot the bombs, but if that guy comes out of the room shoot him."

Who's Rob? Well if Michael is trusting him I will too. Skyler thought then replied to Michael. "Okay, I will be here. Where are you going?"

"If you found a second one that means there could be more. Rob showed me how to defuse these bombs, so if we split up, we can double our chances of getting them all. Oh and, by the way, this one was set to go off at noon. I want you to get out of the buildings and far away. Warn Kax. Rob should be there soon."

Skyler's heart sank. He couldn't imagine what it would do to him if Kax was near one of these bombs. "Shouldn't we sound an alarm or something now that there is more of them?"

"Normally yes, but Rob told me that the Cass have prepared for the bombs to go off to high pitched sounds. So, if we trigger the alarms-"

Skyler cut Michael off. "All goes boom, got it. I think I see Rob, there's a cadet running this way. Talk to you later and good luck." Skyler put the communicator in his pocket. Just as Rob showed up huffing and puffing the Cassiopaean walked out of the room. Skyler aimed his gun. "Stop or I'll shoot!"

The Cassiopaean laughed and hissed, showing his fangs. Ignoring Skyler, it started to walk away.

Rob swiftly went behind the Cassiopaean's and snapped its neck.

Skyler watched in horror. "What was that?"

Rob grinned. "You have never killed a man and you were going to take too long. I have killed so I saved us some time. Now where is the bomb?"

Skyler wasn't sure who to be more worried about the Cassiopaean or Rob. He pointed to the closet.

"Skyler, next Cass you see don't hesitate they are deadlier than you think," Rob went in and quickly defused the bomb. "Pay attention so you can defuse the next one, if need be."

Skyler nodded in shock at how calm Rob seemed to be about this whole situation. "I'll remember that. Who are you by the way?"

Rob held out his seemingly clean hand. "Fifth year Cadet Rob Thorn, now go find Kax and I can handle myself."

How much did Michael tell this guy? He wondered. "I'm heading to Hall B, keep your eyes open for anything else." He ran down the hall. As much as he was worried about Rob, he worried about Kax's safety more.

Running as fast as he could, when he got to the entrance of Hall B he stopped to check the time on his communicator. 11:20 am. *Damn that's close,* he thought. He ran to Kax's classroom. Looking through the window, he didn't see Kax. "Hmm where is she?" he stood around searching.

"Behind you" Kax said standing behind him.

"Why are you here?" Skyler asked confused.

"I was sent as a look out earlier this morning, Cane's orders. I saw you running down the hallway and tried to catch up with you." Kax explained.

Skyler smiled at Kax, "Thanks for being safe."

Kax looked at Skyler. "What happened to this is my last day attitude?"

Skyler smiled at Kax. "There have been a few bombs and it could still be our last day, but I will not let you die. There may be more, if there are more they will go off at noon. I saw one Cass die already."

Her eyes were wide. "Well then I got to get to the hangar and get in my fighter."

Skyler nodded. "Right, let's go."

With their hearts racing they ran down the halls to the hangar.

Skyler checked the time 11:35 am. *Just in time,* he thought.

Kax walked over to the duty computer. She checked logs to sign out her fighter. "Come on, let's go! Cane put a small two-person fighter aside for me. Come on Skyler." She ran to the fighter.

Skyler followed her. He wasn't sure what he was going to do in the fighter with her, but he knew he had to do something.

She got to the fighter and used her code to get in and start the vehicle. While getting it ready, she noticed a group of Cassiopaean enter the hangar. She got out of the fighter and pulled out her gun. She hesitated to shoot.

The Cassiopaean's started to shoot at them.

Skyler pulled out his weapon and just fired in their direction trying to hold them off. "Get going Kax I'll hold them off."

Kax shot a few times. Then jumped back into the fighter. She knew they had to keep going. "What about you? Come with me Skyler."

"Kax you're the pilot. I'll hold them off while you get out of here and do you job." Skyler was keeping them off. He wanted to get into the fighter with Kax but what if there was more and what if they were playing sabotage? He had to stay and fight on the ground. He rushed into the fighter with Kax giving her a big kiss.

She looked at him with shock and worry. "What was that for?"

He smiled. "I'm stealing a kiss for good luck, in case this is the last time we see each other. I'm going to stay on the ground in case there is more. You need to be our eyes in the sky."

Her heart sank. A tear came to her eye.

Skyler wiped her tear away. "Don't cry now I'm still here. I don't want my last thought of you to be a sad one. Cry at my funeral."

Kax gave Skyler a smile right before he closed the fighter's door.

He wondered if that really would be the last time, they would see each other.

***

Michael ran into the hangar just as Kax left. He saw Skyler and the scatter of bodies in the hangar. He stared at Skyler. "You did not go with her?"

Skyler shook his head. "No, there were more things on the ground we needed to worry about. Come on now let's go and find more of those Cass."

Michael looked the time. "No time, we have to run. We have got five minutes before the remaining bombs go off, if any. They already started to evacuate the school once me and Rob warned them that there could be more bombs we did not catch. They sent more to try and get the rest. I told Rob to meet us at the fountain let us go."

Skyler and Michael ran as fast as they could to get outside.

Michael prayed that there weren't anymore bombs and that he and Rob had gotten them all. They ran to the fountain where Rob was waiting for them. Michael checked his watch to see what the time was, 11:58. They got there just in time. Michael pulled out his gun and held on. If the bombs didn't go off who knew what the Cassiopaean's were planning.

Skyler pulled out his gun. He looked at the sky to see if he could see Kax's fighter. She was still flying around to observe and there didn't seem to be anyone else in the air. Then they saw it, Cassiopaean fighters arrived.

In the sky, there were at least twenty of them flying around. It was the attack they were expecting. *But how could Cane expect one little fighter to take on so many,* Skyler thought. Then the fleet showed up, at least seven other fighters appeared all working with Kax. He hoped that she would be okay and that nothing would hurt her. He couldn't live with himself if she were to be injured or worse dead.

The timer went off, Michaels' heart stopped. No bombs went off. Michael waited a bit more just in case his watch was off before he stopped holding his breath. Looking around he tried to see if there were any other signs of the Cassiopaeans besides the battle in the sky.

Rob holding a Cassiopaean blaster that he had taken off one of the bodies, got ready to aim. He looked around prepared to fight and was the first to notice. "Over there!" He said, pointing to the east side of the building.

Skyler pointed to the west side. "There are more on this side."

It was hard to tell from a distance, but the Cassiopaeans had a small army and were going into the buildings with their weapons. There were a few other officers who were going in after them, and they could hear the shots.

Skyler and Rob looked to Michael for a plan.

Michael never thought of himself as a leader type, but this seemed to be the right time to take over and guide them. He looked at both entrances. He looked around then he held out his hand. "Rob you're a good fighter on your own and there seem to be more officers on the east side so go there and knock as many as you can down. Skyler and I will take the west. Got it?"

They both nod and run off in their directions.

Michael and Skyler ran hoping the Cassiopeians were not doing too much damage. They got to the entrance and all the Cassiopaeans were already in there. On the count of three, they entered and just started shooting. The Cassiopaeans was trying to get into the classrooms. The other officers were shooting. Michael and Skyler stayed next to the walls trying not to be hit in the crossfire.

Michael tried to see if he could find a strategy in this. He heard a boom come from the second floor. He stopped what he was doing. "Skyler come with me upstairs, we got to protect Cane."

Without hesitation, Skyler ran back to the entrance of the building and up the stairs. He rushed to Cane's office. But there was a big hole in the floor stopping them.

Commodore Gray stood on the other side with a small glowing cyan tube in his mouth. These tubes exploded like a stick of dynamite when thrown. He took it out and called out to the boys. "The Admiral isn't here, don't worry he is safe. A group of Cassiopaeans came here trying to get close, so I blew them away."

Skyler looked at Michael and whispered. "This guy is nuts."

Michael looked at the giant hole in the floor which he could only assume that dynamite did that. "Yup" he whispered back to Skyler. He could see the floor underneath which did give them an advantage. Michael got on the floor and aimed through the hole at the Cassiopeans.

Skyler copied, trying to get as many Cassiopeans as he could.

Gray joined in, smiling as if he thought this was fun.

The battle raged on. Whenever they got rid of some Cassiopeans there were more coming. They were well prepared for this attack. It was the United Galactic Forces that weren't repaired. Shooting back and forth was tiring and went on and on. But this was a fight till the end, people were dying, and they had to reduce that number as much as they could. They had to keep going till the last Cassiopean was gone.

Chapter 9

Kax returned her fighter to the hangar. She was almost out of fuel by the time the battle had finished. She was lucky that her fighter only got minor damages. She was fine just her nerves were shot. She wondered where Skyler and Michael were. She tried to call them on her communicator, but there were no signals and she feared the worse. She ignored the med techs that were trying to examine her with their handheld medical scanners. She ran to see if she could find out where they were.

She ran out of the hangar looking around outside hoping to find a sign. She looked over at the fountain seeing there was a fighter that had crashed into it. Smashing it to bits making it look more like a pile of stone rubble with water shooting out of it. She could only hope the pilot was safe.

She went to the first hall she came to, Hall A. She walked through the door and saw all the bodies of Cassiopeans and other officers lying on the ground. Trying to make her way through them, she hoped her friends were not there, but she had to know.

A medical crew came through the building looking for anyone who was wounded. She watched two men come in with a stretcher and one walking around to check the bodies. The one man holding the stretcher she recognized as Dr. Kelley.

She knew he was busy, but she had to ask. "Dr. Kelley, have you seen Skyler or Michael?"

He looked up at her from the side of a fallen officer. His face tired and full of grief. "Go to the main hospital they were admitted there awhile go."

Her heart dropped. If they were in the hospital what kind of condition were, they in. She knew better to ask any more questions and just go there and find out. She would not forgive herself if anything happened to her friends. Running out of the building to the hospital she hoped she could find them and hoped they were ok. So many injured people were around it, it was not a nice place to be.

Rushing into the hospital, she saw the overcrowding of injured patients. So many close to death. There was medical staff running all over the place. With all the chaos she tried to grab someone. Finally, she saw a nurse rush past her. Grabbing her shoulder to get her attention. "I'm looking for Cadet Therris and Jones."

The nurse quickly checked her chart and pointed to the wing behind her. "There is a Therris in the first wing I hope he is who you are looking for."

"Thank you." She said and rushed off down the wing. She looked side to side of the row of beds. Some people were badly bleeding, others were missing parts. She couldn't bear to think what condition Skyler was in. She walked slower and slower down the hall, with her worry increasing.

"Oh, come on why did I get a male nurse? I wanted a cute female one." The voice went through the hall.

Kax's heart picked up. She smiled, she knew that voice and cocky attitude. She rushed to the end of the wing. She got to the last curtain. She peeked inside, and her face lit up like the night sky.

Laying on the bed with his left arm in a sling. "Hey Kax, you've finally found me."

Michael standing next to Skyler's bed. "Hey there Kax, glad to see you are in one piece."

Kax rushed up to Michael giving him a hug. "I'm so happy you two are alive and safe, I was so worried once I landed."

Michael hugged back. "We were worried about you too. Fighters are easier to shoot down."

Skyler frowned. "Hey where is my hug? I'm the one who was shot in the shoulder."

Kax went over to Skyler, leaned down and kissed him passionately on the lips.

He moaned enjoying her soft lips. "What was that for?"

"You stole a kiss from me before this attack started for good luck. Now that it's over I'm taking it back." She winked.

Chapter 10

RING RING! Skyler rolled over grabbing his phone off the nightstand. "Ahh," he winced as he answered the call.

"Skyler are you alright?" Asked the voice on the other line.

Sitting up in a comfortable position. "Ya, I'm alright uncle Justin. My shoulder just hurts is all."

"What happened to your shoulder?" Justin asked.

"There was an attack on the base and I kinda got shot. It's a minor wound, it has been a few days and it's mostly healed. It's just sore now." Skyler tried to flex the arm.

"I know this is your dream and you're doing what you love, but I do worry about you too."

"I know, and I will be fine." He put the phone on speaker so he could rub his injured shoulder.

"I'm calling to let you know I spoke to David on the phone and we have agreed to meet at the cabin on Friday. Does that work for you?"

"Well, with the attack, classes have been reduced until they fix up some of the buildings. But I think Friday would be an okay day." Skyler reached over to grab his tablet. He turned it on and looked through his schedule.

"It wouldn't be until the afternoon or late evening anyway, so I hope you are home. I would love to see where you are living and meet your friends. Might I ask why you would like to buy this house. It wasn't clear in the e-mail you sent me."

Skyler sighed. "I want to buy it for Kax. She's this real special girl I met in my first year here and she has let me, and Michael stay up here many times. Her family can't afford this place anymore and it means a lot to her. I really just want to buy it for her. But I don't think she will accept a big gift like that from me. So, I'll keep it but it's for her."

"Does she know how you feel and why you are doing this?"

"She knows how I feel. But she thinks I'm just buying this house to be nice. She's not interested in me." He let out a long sigh.

"I understand. Well maybe you shouldn't be wasting your time with her. There are other options out there. I could always hook you up with someone if you're ready to settle down."

Skyler rolled his eyes. "Not this again. I told you and Angelica's father I'm not going to marry her."

"Angelica got married earlier this year to the Earl of Kensington. I was talking about other girls."

Skyler's heart sank. Angelica was his first serious girlfriend. He spent the summer with her in England when he was sixteen. Her father wanted to arrange a marriage for them, but he was too young, and career focused. "Well I'm happy for her. You can tell her that when you see her again."

"You know I will. Is there anything else?"

Skyler shook his head. He didn't feel much like talking now. "No, I think that's everything."

"I'll see you Friday then."

Chapter 11

Friday arrived and Kax was getting the house ready for her father's visit. She had spoken to him, making sure he was still coming. He had been worried about her and even if he weren't to sell the house, he would have liked to have seen her. She missed her dad, they were always close but since she joined the academy there time together had been cut. She was just finishing tidying up when she heard someone at the door.

David used his key to open the door of the log cabin. Stepping in he called out. "Hello, Kax, I'm here."

Kax rushed upstairs to greet her father. She didn't see him, but she heard his voice in the distance.

"What the heck are you doing?"

Kax ran to the kitchen where she heard her father shout. She entered the kitchen and she shook her head.

Skyler was frying up a few burgers in his boxers.

Michael was stopped with a bowl of salad in his hands. "Hello, you must be Mr. Tillion, glad to meet you."

Skyler put the spatula down and held out his hand. "Hey David, nice to see you again."

David scowled at Skyler. "It's Mr. Tillion to you and put on some pants."

Taken back by his words he laughed. "I was just waiting for my clothes to dry. They should be ready about now. Please excuse me." Skyler left the room.

"I warned him, I have been trying to get him to put pants on all day." Michael said.

David stared at Michael. "Please tell me you and he are together because I don't want him dressed like that near my daughter."

Michael sighed waving his hand. "No, we are not, and Skyler is harmless he is just a bit eccentric. Kax knows how to deal with him."

"Skyler is not worth the effort Daddy." Kax said standing behind her father.

David turned around and hugged his daughter. "I'm so happy you are alive and safe."

"I'm fine Daddy don't worry." Letting go of her father, she looked at him. "So, I guess you have met Michael and Skyler?"

David groaned. "I have never been one to tell you who you can't hang out with. But darling, are you sure these are people you want to be hanging out with?"

Kax frowned. "Now dad I know Skyler is a bit eccentric, but he is a good guy. Michael is as safe as they come."

David sighed. "I just worry about you is all. Do you want me to help set things up?"

She shook her head. "No, I will finish this, and you can just sit and relax you're the guest here."

David sat down at the table watching his daughter set it. "So how is school going?"

***

Skyler now wearing a green T-shirt and faded blue jeans finished cooking up the last of the burgers. The music was off and this time, when he heard the knock at the door. He turned the burner off and went to the door. Opened it to saw his uncle Justin. "Hey, Uncle glad you could make it."

He looked Skyler over. "How is your shoulder doing?"

Skyler rubbed his shoulder. "Still hurts a bit doctor, I was was able to use a cell regenerator on it to help speed up the healing. It might leave a bit of a scar, but I can use it."

The white-haired balding man adjusted his small round glasses and looked at the shoulder. "Well as long as you can use it that's all that is important. I didn't tell your mother. Is Mr. Tillion here yet?"

Skyler pointed, "He is on the patio. Just go through the hall and out the glass doors to the deck. Thanks, mom is the last person I want knowing."

Justin made his way to see David.

Skyler walked back to the kitchen to help with the last of the food preparations. Took the burgers out of the pan and onto a plate.

David stood up from the kitchen table. "Hello, you must be Mr. Munroe, I'm David Tillion. it's so nice to meet you."

Justin shook the blonde Catillion's hand. "Call me Justin, it is a pleasure to meet you too. Should we get down to business now or after we eat?"

David looked in the kitchen and out on the patio. "After, I think the meal is just about ready."

Skyler and Michael began to carry the food to the patio.

Justin and David got up and followed them out.

Kax sat on the other side of her father while the boys placed the food on the table.

Skyler sat down next to his uncle and Michael at the end of the table between Kax and Skyler.

On the table, there were burgers and salad. More than enough for everyone. All took their burgers and what they wanted of the garden salad.

Skyler impatiently went to eat his burger as soon as it hit the plate.

Michael cleared his throat. "I know I may be the only Christian here, but I would like us to say grace before we eat."

They all looked at him in awe.

Justin nodded. "That's sounds like a good idea, would you do us the honors, Mr. Jones."

Michael got them to all hold hands and started. "Thank you, God, for this food we are about to receive. Thank you for bringing us all here together on this lovely sunny day, Amen."

Once done they all started eating.

Justin looked at Michael's strange appearance. "Might I ask, how does that work you're a Squallite and a Christian?"

Michael looked up from his salad. "When my father came to Earth, he adopted the Earth customs and even their old religion that is how I am Catholic."

Justin took a bite of his salad. "Interesting my wife is Christian only because of the traditions of the British monarchy. So, I'm used to things even though I'm not one of them."

David looked over at Justin. "I'm curious I heard you're married to a Duchess, but you don't go by Duke why is that?"

Justin lightly smiled. "I get that a lot. My wife holds her own title and I'm just a commoner. Normally our marriage wouldn't be allowed but she was married once before because of duty reasons and is widowed and so for her second marriage she could marry me without losing her title. She carries the title I don't. If roles were reversed, I would be a Duke. I still go to all the parties and functions with her. I have offered Skyler a chance to marry into the family a few times, but he has turned me down."

Skyler rolled his eyes. "Uncle I was sixteen, I don't want to marry, not yet. what's the difference between those girls and anyone else?"

Kax watched Skyler as he talked.

"The difference is Skyler you will have money and power. Also, now you are doing your time in the Galactic Forces would really look impressive. There are many fine young noble women in the royal family you have a chance with."

Skyler looked at Kax. "I'm sure they are nice, but I have what I want right now. I'm on my way to becoming a captain and that will give me all the money and power I need."

David cuts in. "What about a wife?"

Skyler's face went red. "Well I have someone in mind, but there is plenty of time to find one later if that one doesn't work out."

Justin cut in. "Which is all the more reason to marry a royal you don't have to see her because you are working and once you find someone else you can divorce, just as long as you give her a child to carry the title."

Skyler shifted uncomfortably in his seat. "Now you want me to have kids. Uncle, I appreciate this, but I'm sorry. I have other plans for now, if I change my mind, I will call you."

David cut in. "So, Justin what do you think of this place?"

Justin turned in his chair to look at what he could see of the outside of the house. "From what I have seen, it is a fine place and if my nephew wants it, I will get it for him. I will still buy it today, but I'm having a house inspector come out next week to check how good of condition the house is in. Normally I would do this all before, but I'm a busy man and as long as it is not a shack, I have no problem with my nephew living here with your daughter."

David sipped his glass of water.

Michael cleared his throat. "I am living here too."

David smiled. "I'm so glad about that you are sharing a bed with Skyler and he's not with my daughter."

Skyler and Michael shifted a little away from each other. "No, we are not." Skyler and Michael both replied at the same time.

Kax face went flush. "Skyler and Michael are just friends they're not a couple. But we all have separate rooms, Michael has the middle room I have the master. We all have our own rooms."

"I told you earlier Mr. Tillion there is nothing between me and Skyler." Michael blurted out.

Justin frowned. "I'm confused what is the loving arrangement here? Skyler, I thought you told me Kax was your consort? But David is saying Michael is?"

Skyler covered his face as the whole table stared at him with angry and confused faces. "Okay before any of you get mad at me, let me explain. I like Kax yes, but she is just a friend who I have feelings for. Michael is not my boyfriend, he's just my roommate from the academy and good friend. Nothing has happened between any of us. We are just good friends. We all have different rooms and take care of our needs in our own ways."

David glared at Skyler with suspicion.

"Well now that that's cleared up." Justin pulled out his checkbook out of his suit pocket. "How much do you want me to make this out for?"

David pulled the copy of the deed out of jacket pocket. "What I told you on the phone just the last appraised value."

Justin wrote the cheque, tore it off and handed it to David, "There it is and a little extra. To cover the taxes and fees."

David took the cheque and signed the deed over to Justin. He handed him the deed. "Thank you so much sir."

Justin took the deed and handed it to Skyler. He got out of his seat, straightened his jacket. "Thank you for the lovely meal, but I must be off I have to catch a flight to England."

Skyler stood up. "You're leaving so soon? If you're leaving who is at your local house?"

Justin headed to the door. "No one right now but if you want to pick up the rest of your stuff you can go there anytime doesn't matter if you have your key, front gate knows you."

Skyler got out of his seat and walked with his uncle to the front door of the house. "Thank you for everything."

Justin turned and looked straight into his nephew's eyes. "Skyler you're my only Nephew. You are the only thing to take this family into the next generation. I will do anything I can for you. That girl Kax is a nice girl I hope you take care of her. Girls like that are rare to find. But you can't force anything, don't waste too much time on her and pass up something better. And no judgment if you wanted someone like Michael, he seems like a good guy too."

Skyler rubbed the back of his neck and let out an embarrassed laugh. "Thanks again. For your advice but I can manage my own love life."

Justin gave his nephew a hug. "Take care of yourself."

***

Later in the night after everyone left, Skyler was getting ready for bed. Undressing in his room he looked out the window. All that he could see was trees, but it was better than no window at all. A knock came to his door. Confused he said. "Come in."

Kax walked into the room still fully dressed. "Hey Skyler, I want to talk to you."

Skyler went and sat on his bed. "Sure, talk to me all you want."

Kax took a deep breath. "I know you are a nice guy and I know you like me but what is the real reason you bought this house? Was it for me?"

Skyler sighed. "I didn't want to see you unhappy. Kax I don't want you thinking it was because I'm hitting on you or I want to use it against you. I did it because this house means something important to you. I can tell by the look in your eyes that when you're here you feel close to your mother and it is a museum of all the memories of her." He got up and went to the closet and pulled out the box with blue tape. He put it on the bed and pulled out a wooden box with a marble-sized pure dark violet crystal ball inside. He took the ball out and handed it to Kax. "That crystal is a Corsair stone. There're only about 200 of them in the galaxy and that is a big one. They come from Caprican space and are given only to the Pirate Captains. That stone is worth a lot more than this house. I could sell it, but the story behind it means more than all the money in the world to me."

Kax played with the crystal in her hand. "It's so lovely, what is the story about?"

Skyler smiled. "My dad told me the story, it was before he married my mother. He was a young captain and was on a trade mission in Caprica and while he was there, he ran into problems with pirates and ended up saving this woman's life she turned out to be the king's daughter and for a reward she gave him the stone. He didn't know what it was at first and she told him that it was a Corsair stone and that he had the heart of a Pirate and it was only fitting that this stone goes to one. He took it as a compliment and held on to it as a good luck charm. He used to tell me the story before I went to bed. I don't care how much this stone is worth it holds too many memories I could never part with it."

Kax handed the crystal back to Skyler. "So, you're really just a nice guy?"

He put the stone back into the box and placed the box on the nightstand. "Well, this is information I have never told anyone else in my life, so you better not go blabbing it. So, enjoy your house."

She leaned over to Skyler, wrapping her arms around him giving him a hug. "Thank you."

Chapter 12

Two weeks had passed since the attack. Enough of the school had been rebuilt so all classes could resume. The green grass that once covered the grounds was no more. They had been torn up and replaced by mounds of dirt. The buildings that once stood proud and tall were now covered in blast marks and making them age well before there time. This did not look like the friendly place it once was but didn't look like the desiccant remains of a war zone.

Skyler drove the car past the grounds. He was saddened to see the damage that had been done. To the place, he called home and loved so dearly. He pulled into his parking spot and got out of the car. With Kax by his side, they walked into the class to see how the rest of the buildings looked. The main structures of these buildings were still standing and had been repainted. It was the appearance that was unsightly. They needed to be repainted and cleaned up. For now, the forces were just concerned about getting the cadets back in classes and making the base operational.

Moving down the halls, he headed to Cane's office. They hadn't heard from him since the attack, they hoped that was a good thing. Skyler and Kax made there way down the halls. The big hole in the floor had been repaired so you wouldn't have to worry about falling through. Skyler opened the door to Cane's office.

The secretary was sitting at her desk, she looked up at them. "Fleet Admiral Cane is not in today, please come back later."

Thinking this is odd Skyler frowned. "Well, where is he? He hasn't answered the phone in two weeks?"

The secretary looked Skyler over. "Listen Cadet Therris I know you know the Fleet Admiral well, so I will tell you this. He is gone to Lyra city for a bit, no idea when he will be back. Don't tell anyone, it's top-secret. If you are wondering about the guns you are carrying, he wants you to keep wearing them you never know when we will have another attack. If you really need to see someone about how the school is run, Fleet Admiral Thompson is the only one on Earth Base. But Admiral Judson and Admiral Marlow are taking care of a lot of the stuff in the repairs department."

His heart sunk while he listened, he wondered. *Why was Cane in Lyra that was right in the edge of the borderlands.* "Thank you for the info we should be fine." Skyler turned and walked out of the room with Kax following behind. Without a word, Skyler singled for Kax to follow him into the closest bathroom, located down the hall. Before saying anything, he looked in all the stalls for people or bugs.

"What are you doing Skyler? Why are we here?" she asked.

The room was clean. "Okay Kax your people are near Lyra. I want to know what would Cane be doing in such a dangerous spot?"

Kax leaned on the counter and rolled her eyed. "Skyler, Lyra is not near me or the Broadlands. Study your star charts more. I don't know why he is there? Makes no sense to me as the Lyrian's are humanoid traders known for their fashion skills and hospitality. Lyra City is more of a tourist place, they don't even have an army. Maybe it's just a place to hide out. I would only be worried if he was in Cepheus City because that's really on the edge of the borderlands and has a high Cass population but still part of our federation. I think that's the place you were thinking of."

Skyler smacked his forehead. "Damnit your right. How could I get those two confused?" Skyler leaned on the counter and rubbed his chin. "Something is up is all I can say. Why abandon the fleet when this is the time, he is needed the most, just to go on vacation?"

Kax shook her head. "He hasn't abandoned the fleet. Davis is gone too. Thompson has more experience. He is the one who is needed. He can give orders and control all fleets at once. Cane and

Davis are probably being just being protected. That way if one falls, we're not hopeless and there will be another."

Skyler brushed his hair back. "I guess your right I'm just paranoid. Thanks for clearing things up with me."

Kax smiled and headed towards the door of the bathroom.

"Wait, Kax, you want to steal a ship and take a few weeks off and go to Lyra City?"

She turned around and frowned at Skyler. "You got the money to buy a ticket, no stealing. Skyler, things will be all right. You will have plenty of time to go travel space when you're a captain."

He walked to the door. "Ya, I guess your right, I just worry sometimes."

***

Lunch time, Michael had got off class earlier this time and was able to get a full meal instead of just a fruit cup. He sat down at a table with his garden salad and fruit cup. He started to eat while he waited for the rest of the gang.

Skyler and Kax made their way to the table with their lunch trays.

"Lunch is good today, replicated Salisbury steak is the special," Skyler wasted no time digging into his food.

Kax had ordered the same. She looked at Michael's salad. "Are you enjoying your salad?"

Michael finished his mouthful of food. "Yes, it is really fresh I like this new cafeteria. But this is the one part of the school that does not seem to be upgraded."

Kax looked down at her pocket tablet. "Well according to the e-mail sent out by the Academy they plan to be doing a lot of upgrades over the next while."

Skyler frowned. "That makes no sense we are at war. Why would they care about upgrades when the Cass are just going to blow this place apart again?"

Michael shifted his eyes. "Only thing I can think of is they plan to fill the buildings with more defense, or it is a distraction. But they are also going to be closing it next year to do all these things at once. I guess we are all getting off-world postings unless anyone wants go to Siberia or the Sahara."

Skyler groaned. "Too hot, too cold. I'll take the off-world one. Those bases are good for science officers, engineers or security. I'd be wasting my time doing command training there."

"Maybe I will get accepted for deep space training and be posted to Catillion." Kax put her tablet away. "It would be nice if we had a distraction around here."

Michael picked at his salad. "I think to prevent ourselves from going bonkers about this war we just try and live our normal lives. We all know we could use a little normal. I think I might just go spend some time with my dad. Especially if we are going to have to relocate next year. There is no way I could afford the transporter credits from here to Siberia weekly."

Skyler focused his attention to Michael. "How is your dad doing?"

Michael curved his mouth. "He is doing a lot better. Dr. Kelley was able to find a way to trick his body into thinking it is not aging. He is due to go back to work tomorrow. So, I will try and get some more time with him."

Kax smiled. "That's great to hear you have fun with your dad. It is a new school year and things have been crazy since we got here it's time for us to have fun before the next attack."

Skyler quickly finished his lunch, pulling out of his pocket the keys to his car. Sliding them across the brown table to Kax. "Speaking of having fun, I have a date tonight."

Kax took the keys. "So, you aren't going to be at the house tonight and neither is Michael. What am I supposed to do?"

A sly smile crossed Skyler's face. "Well you could have your own fun. If you want, you can join me? Nancy is a really nice girl who is really open I'm sure she wouldn't mind-"

"Stop right there I don't want to hear any more about this. My answer is no and don't ask again." Her eyes flared with rage.

Skyler leaned back in his seat, waving his hands. "Sorry, I'll ask someone else."

Michael finished his lunch. "Well I am off. Nice seeing you. Not sure if I should pretend not to know you anymore Skyler. If Kax kills you I will go to your funeral, but I will not wear black. Till next time, bye." He took his tray and left the cafeteria.

Kax laughed at Michael's comment. "Lunch is about over. I guess I will see you tomorrow then."

"Kax what did I say wrong?" He asked before she left.

"I know you weren't serious, but you just triggered another thing from my past. I'm not mad but just drop it." She took her tray and walked away.

***

Skyler sat at the lunchroom table by himself. He picked at his food. Worrying about Kax. *Damn I said the wrong thing again. I wonder what that guy did to her. I hate men who abuse and treat women like that.* He took his time finishing his food.

"Is this seat taken?" Asked a familiar voice.

Skyler looked up and with a smile. "Perry, there you are, long time no see. Where have you been?"

Perry had some dirt on his forehead and sat down across form Skyler. On his tray was a rainbow gelatin-based food. "Plants. Spent my summer and the last month genetically altering plants. I haven't had much time to get out. I rarely get to leave for lunch. I'm lucky I found you. Your name isn't in the dorm directory anymore."

"Me, Michael and Kax moved to the cabin. But you could have called my number is the same."

Perry scratched his head. "Yeah about that. I lost my communicator. A couple of months back in a plant. Waiting for it to bloom so I can get it back."

"You are so weird." Skyler finished off his plate. "So where have you been living?"

"In the basement of engineering. There is a greenhouse lab there. I keep putting in complaints that we need more sunlight and that the artificial solar lamps are not enough, but they don't listen. I do have a dorm, I think? I haven't been there. I work so long of hours I just nap next to the plants."

"Dude I could not do what you do. How long do you plan to keep this up?"

"Until we get the results we're looking for. Michael sends me the math and I do my best to make it work. Good news is this is counting as my schoolwork and some extra credit so I'm not missing anything."

Skyler raised a puzzled eyebrow. "You have been talking to Michael?"

Perry shook his head. "Not directly. He just e-mails me in new formulas based on the results I send him. In other news, what's news, how was Squall and what's up with you and Kax?"

"We're just friends. Squall was okay I felt like I was wasting a summer and based on the reports Cane has placed me in some diplomacy classes. Also, I got banned from returning. Did you hear the base is closing next year?"

Perry ate away at his food. "Oh yeah, Admiral Green is going to monitor my progress and if I need more time, he is thinking of posting me to Catillion."

"You too? Kax mentioned about going there too. Maybe I should plan to go there. I always thought of finishing my command training on Tauroton."

"Have you looked at the program there? You're stubborn enough as it is, you don't need to learn from those bull heads. Catillion wouldn't be too bad. From what I have heard it's a different style of command that you might benefit from."

"I'll consider what you say. But I got to go. I have one class this afternoon and then I have a date." Skyler took his tray. "What is that thing you're eating anyway?"

"It's protein jelly. I must be very careful what I eat around the new plants. Certain body odors and gasses can affect the chemical balance. So, I'm on a strict diet."

"You're so weird. See you later buddy." Skyler waved goodbye to his friend.

Chapter 13

With the night to herself, Kax decided to take her time going home and check on some other friends of hers. She called the number she had for Jake and Ron assuming they had a different dorm this year.

Jake answered his communicator. "Kax, is that you?"

She smiled into the phone. "Yup I'm back from Squall and thought I would check in on you guys."

Jake sighed into the phone. "It's been a rough couple of months for us. Are you free tonight? Want to stop by the barracks and catch up?"

"Barracks did you graduate?" She asked.

"Unfortunately, I did. I'll message you the room number."

A short time later Kax knocked on the door. She stepped back when she saw Jake's face.

"Hello Kax, please come in." He stepped aside for her to enter the room. On his left side of his had a scar tissue that looked to be from a burn and his eye drooped.

"What happened to you? Is that from the attack? Where is Ron?"

"Sit down." He pointed to the bed. "It's a long story that's why I invited you over." The barracks were slightly bigger than the dorms. With a double bed to one side of the wall. A full built closet, computer desk across from the end of the bed. There was table and chairs with a little kitchenette.

She sat down at the kitchen table. "Is that scar from the attack?"

"I wish." Jake scoffed taking a seat across from her at the table. "Ron's on medical leave and me I'm never going to be normal again."

"Wait didn't Ron's surgery go well?"

Jake shook his head. "At first it did but then he got an infection. His bones couldn't adapt to the change. So, he's living in the hospital until they can figure out how to adapt his body. He might die in there."

"That's horrible." A tear came to her eye.

"As for me, when I went to get my ears fixed and I had a reaction to the drugs, and it caused an infection which has left this scaring and nerve damage." Jake said with a sigh.

"Don't they have way to correct the damage?" Kax said with concern in her voice.

Jake shook his head. "Not really. They do for humans but not really for Squallite's. But the Forces won't cover me no more because I have had too many surgeries in my time here that they are deeming cosmetic and not medical that if I want anymore done, I have to pay for them myself."

"Do you not have the money?"

"The money isn't the issue. It's finding a plastic surgeon. In the forces, a lot was no questions just fill out the paperwork. But now finding my own I need a Squallite for a few things and they will not do it and with a human, I might have worse reactions. My transition is at a standstill right now." He got up and went over to the kitchen and picked up two teacups. "Would you like some orange tea?"

"Orange Pekoe?"

"No orange Squallite tea. Have you ever had it?" Jake asked.

"Yes, I had some this summer it was nice. Sure, I would love a glass."

Jake took two teabags out and placed them in the cups with some water. Then placed them on the heating pad and set the timer. "They will be ready soon."

"I'm really sorry about your surgeries. I had high hopes for you."

Jack scoffed. "So, did I. So many things have changed in the time I have met you." He rubbed his brown hairs out of his face. Tears began to form in his eyes oval eyes making them seem their original orange.

The timer on the tea went. Kax got up and took the two cups and turned the heating pad off. She placed the two cups on the table and then went over to Jake. She put her arms around him. "It will be ok you will figure this all out and move on. I believe you will be human one day."

"Kax it isn't just about being human. I want my life back. I want my life with Ron back. I love him and now he is in a hospital bed dying. I'm an officer on the frontlines and this is all not going as planned." He took a sip of his tea. "For Squallites it is said this tea has healing properties, but I have been drinking it non-stop for weeks now and I'm not feeling any different."

Kax went to go and sit down back down.

"Kax would you do me a favor and stay with me here tonight?" He sighed. "I'm tired of being alone. I just want some comfort."

She looked around the room. "Jake you only have one bed."

"Does that bother you? You don't have to stay." He went back to drinking his tea.

Jake's a good friend he needs someone and isn't trying to be a creep. I know him. She nodded her head. "I got no one waiting for me, I'm free tonight."

He smiled. "Thank you Kax, you're a good friend."

***

Late into the night Kax was awoken by Jake's tossing and turning. She placed her hand on Jake's bicep. "Jake wake up you're having a bad dream!"

He opened his eyes, the orange behind the blue coloring still glowing orange. "Kax it was horrible. I had a dream Ron died and I was kicked out of the forces and things just kept getting worse. Thank you for being by my side. I sometimes hate that I trained myself because now I have terrible dreams. I sometimes wish I could just go back to being in a equality meditate trans but then I would hate myself for acting like... a Squallite."

"I'm sorry," She reached over and turned on the lamp that was next to the bed. She hugged him. "You will be fine Jake. Everything will be fine. You have me by your side."

He leaned in and kissed her on the lips. "Thank you."

She pushed back. "Jake what are you doing?"

He stopped for a second and rubbed his hand through his hair. "Oh gosh, Kax, I'm sorry. I don't know what I was thinking. I'm sorry. That wasn't my plan or intention-"

She kissed him back. "It's okay Jake I understand."

"You're an amazing person and I'm glad you came into my life." He kissed her again rubbing his hand through her hair. "I'll be gentle."

"Thank you." She rolled on top of him. Kissing him repeatedly.

Chapter 14

Skyler laid back in the bed. He rolled over and smiled at the lovely cat-eared beauty next him. Kissing her juicy cherry lips gave him such pleasure. "So, Nancy, how was I?"

She rolled her figures up and down his chest, playing with his soft baby like chest hairs. "You're getting better, still a few tricks you need to improve on."

He had too much bliss to be upset. "You'd think after three months of these weekly sessions I would be an expert by now. Are you just trying to keep me around?" He shifted on top of her kissing down her neck.

She purred, moving her hands up and down his back. "Well maybe it is just me," she whispered into his ear.

The door in the dorm opened and a purple-haired female human walked through the door. "I thought you said he would be gone in the morning?"

Skyler quickly shifted, sitting up using the blanket to cover himself.

Nancy slowly grabbed the robe of the corner of her bed and slipped it on. "He will be gone. Sorry, we slept in. Don't worry we're done for now." She leaned down and handed Skyler his shirt and pants.

Skyler struggled to put them on under the covers. Once on he got off the bed, he picked up his gun and shoes.

The purple-haired science cadet frowned. "If you get caught with him here, I'm not taking any of the blame."

Nancy rolled her eyes ignoring her roommate's warning. "Hey Skyler, instead of meeting on Tuesday how about we meet also this Friday. I have a new girlfriend who is interested in trying out a human male and told her about you. She's eighteen and a first year Medical Cadet, also a Catillion. You will like her."

A charming smiling came over his face. "Well I look forward to meeting her and I will be here." He finished putting on his clothes.

The roommate snapped. "Friday you're going to have two people in the room, you already bend the rules with having a guy here, but now you want two people here?"

Nancy rolled her head stretching her neck. She went over to her roommate, placing her hands on her roommate's face. "You need to get laid more, Mandy." She kissed her on the lips.

Skyler watched as he headed to the door.

Nancy waved to him as he left.

He walked down the hall, checking his pocket tablet he had fifteen minutes to get to class. *Tuesday morning, that's O'Brien's with Kax, perfect I almost forgot.* He rushed through the halls to get to class.

He got there with not a minute to spare. Because of the war, there was less time spent in the classroom and more in the battle simulators. He went to the lineup with the rest of the class. He stood next to Kax.

She looked him over. "You're later than normal, I guess someone had a fun night."

He let out a soft smile and laugh. "Ya, you could say that but good news I will be home tonight got nothing planned."

Kax shook his head. "Well it would be nice to see you more than just weekends."

Skyler smirked. "Am I hearing you right? Do you miss me?"

Rolling her eyes. "Only in your dreams. But it is your place too and you should use it."

O'Brien walked into the room stopping Skyler and Kax's preclass conversation. "Okay class, today we are going to learn what to do in case there is a raid."

Skyler raised his hand. "Sir we learned that last week and the week before isn't there anything else we need to learn?"

O'Brien walked over to Skyler looking him dead in the eyes. "You're right." He walked up and down the lineup of Cadets. "There isn't much more the teach you, kids. We have been training every other day and there hasn't been an attack. Most of you are passing this easy now. I normally would be showing you how to fight and attack a ship, but orders from the higher-ups is to teach you only hand-to-hand simulations. I wouldn't say this about all of my classes, but you cadets are ready to go."

Kax spoke up. "Sir if we know all this why you don't teach us what to do if this does happen on a ship. This war has just begun and most of us will graduate this or next year and being put on ships so teach us to be prepared for the future."

O'Brien turned and smiled at Kax. "I like the way you think, lass. So, let's get started. We will try one scenario and the another. All crew into your positions."

***

Sitting at his workstation, Cadet Thorn stood behind Michael and watched him while he worked. Michael turned his head and looked right into Thorn's dark dead eyes. "Is there something I can help you with?"

Rob put on a devilish smile. "You have been very suspicious of me since that attack almost three months ago. You know I helped save your life I think that makes us friends."

Michael continued to study and watch Rob's soulless eyes. "It does but since that day being around you gives me and uneasy feeling."

Rob chuckled. "I do that to a lot of people. But I told you before I have killed people. Once you kill a few, life doesn't mean the same."

Shaking his head. "I guess it wouldn't. We can be friends and thank you for saving mine and my friends' lives. I guess I shouldn't be too hard on you."

Giving a crooked smile back. "Thanks, that means a lot to me. Can I hang with you and your friends at lunch?"

Michael shrugged. "I guess so it could not hurt." Michael turned back in his seat, pulling out a textbook and reading. He could sense Rob was still watching him, it sent shivers down his spine. Trying to focus on his work. He said without turning around in his seat. "Okay Rob I can tell you are still standing behind me, please explain why?"

A devilish smile crossed his face. He leaned down looking over Michael's shoulder. "I don't care how you choose to learn but if I'm correct that's a command textbook and it's illegal for you to have one, let alone touch it?"

Michael closed the book turning to look at Rob. "I think you have noticed this is an unconventional classroom."

Rob whispered in his ear. "In these class walls it might be okay, but you like to take that book out of the classroom."

Glaring into Rob's eyes. "It is my roommate's book, I return it to him when I am done. If I get caught, I am willing to deal with that. Even if it gets me thrown out. So, what do you want?"

"Just as long as you know what you're getting into cadet." Rob grinned and walked away.

With his heart racing, he closed the book and placed it back into his bag.

Commodore Gray went to the right side of Michael's workstation. "You can have the book don't let what Thorn says bother you."

Looking up at Gray, he sighed. "The fewer people know the better."

82

Gray placed his hand on Michael's shoulder. "I wish there was more like you. You can't be successful if you don't take risks. I give this free study work time for people to think out of the box and that is just what you are doing. Take time to learn it all."

Chapter 15

Sitting at the lunch table, Skyler was reading a letter on his pocket tablet while trying to eat his lunch. He looked up from the letter when he noticed Kax and Michael sat down at the table. "Hey, Kax did you get the e-mail were getting medals."

Kax sat down and took the tablet right out of Skyler's hands. Reading the letter then she handed it back. She pulled out her tablet to see if she got anything. She found her letter too.

Michael checked his. "It appears we are all getting medals."

Kax looked at her letter reading it over. "Wait I'm getting a Sliver Spark. I think Skyler is getting a Blue Star of Bravery."

Michael checked on his tablet. "I am getting a Blue Star too, but I think the reason you're getting a different medal is because that is a Pilot's medal."

Skyler looked at the letter. "We should all also be getting our service medals for last summer when we were on Squall and the mission ones too."

Finishing his bite of salad. "We don't get two for the mission on Squall we get the 149GA Squall service medal with a gold medallion on it and not silver like the other ones because we were on a secret mission not so secret now that were back, and it worked. But we are overdue for them."

Kax ate her food. "Well, at least, when we are on Squall, they gave you that inventors medal before they forgot."

Skyler looked over the time for the ceremony. "Sweet we get Monday off school."

Kax looked at the time on her letter. "We have the day off because the ceremony is at noon. Not everyone is getting medals, why are they canceling the whole day?"

Rob came over to the table with his lunch and sat next to Kax. "Because it is a distraction. They only do things like this to cover up what they are really doing."

Skyler looked at Rob. "You're that guy who helped out in the attack. Are you getting a medal too?"

Rob's mouth widened. "Yes, I am and well I did help you so of course. It's nice to see you all again."

"So, Rob, where did you meet Michael?" Kax shifted away from Rob who was, sitting a little too close.

"We have a class together." He held out his hand. "You must be Kax the lovely pilot who Skyler is so smitten with."

Kax shook his hand and turned her attention to Michael. "What have you told him about me?"

Michael's eyes widened and froze. "I did not say anything about you and Skyler."

Rob snickered. "No one told me but during the attack, I could see how worried Skyler was. It reminded me of my brother when he first met his wife."

Her face turned pink like a cherry blossom, letting out a nervous laugh. "Oh, is that so." She looked over at Skyler to see his reaction.

He shrugged his shoulders, covering half his face. "Well, I guess some feelings are harder to turn off than others."

Rob shook his head. "She's your weakness, that's your problem. I know you were trying to be macho, but sometimes you got to put that aside."

Kax cleared her throat. "I'm sitting right here."

"It's not like that, Rob. I care about Kax like I care about Michael and Perry." He snapped back.

Rob grinned at the mention of Perry's name. "You know Perry Zyrix?"

"Ya, he was my roommate one summer, what's it to you?" Skyler's suspicion grew.

"Nothing just didn't realize you knew him." Rob ate three French fries off his tray.

The environment of the table changed. There was now a cold chill surrounding them. They all felt awkward and didn't know what to say next.

Rob finished his food while humming a symphonic tune. "Well that was a nice meal let's do this again sometime." He picked up his tray and walked away.

Kax waited till Rob was gone then shifted closer to Michael. "Not to insult your friend but he was creepy."

"You get that feeling about him too? I thought it was just me." Michael sighed.

"Creepy? That guy puts the crypt in crypt keeper. You mentioned to me that he once killed somebody before the day of the attack, do you know who that person was?" Skyler blurted out.

"I saw him kills a Cass without blinking an eye during the attack but who he killed before I hav no idea."

Kax took Michael's hand. "Please ask him. I think that might help explain his attitude."

"Ya, like what if the people he killed were his last group of friends." Skyler spoke with a mouthful of food.

Michael rolled his eyes. "I am certain that is not the case. It probably is not as bad as you think."

Kax and Skyler looked at each other skeptically.

Chapter 16

"Thanks for coming along. I could use a woman's advice." Skyler said driving into the city looking at Nancy in the seat next to him.

Tossing her hair in the open wind of the coverable. "Anything to ride in your car, Skyler. But why do you need to get Kax a gift? What did you do?"

"Nothing I just want to do something nice as a housewarming gift." Driving faster in the car. "I didn't know you wanted to go for a ride in my car so much. You should have asked sooner. Want to have some fun in it after were done today?"

She leaned in close and put his hand on this thigh. "Maybe we will see where things go."

He pulled up to the strip mall, parking near a flower shop. "Do flowers really make women feel special?"

"Yes, I think this will be a great housewarming gift for Kax." Nancy laughed placing her hand on Skyler's shoulder as they walk into the store. "You have lots to learn."

Inside the store, Skyler looked at all the different kinds of flowers. He saw some that were pink miniature roses. "Do you think she will like these they're roses girls like roses."

Nancy rolled her eyes, pulling his arm away from them. She took him to these sparkling purple and gold lilies. "Get her these they're native to hers and my planet and they are rare a few of these she will love you."

Skyler leaned in to smell one of the flowers. Nancy pulled him away. "Only the person you give them to is allowed to smell them up close that is a tradition."

They went to the counter and checked out. Normally he would have hit the ceiling with knowing how much just six of theses flower's cost, but this was for Kax.

Walking out the building to put the flowers in the car. "So, what would be the best way to give them to her?"

Nancy laughed. "Since they are a housewarming gift, I would recommend that when you get home, place them in a vase and set them on the table with a lovely card. Simple but she will love it."

BOOM! BOOM! A large explosion came from somewhere behind the mall. Skyler looked up in the sky. He saw a couple of Cassiopaean fighters circling above. The city was under attack. Fighters circled the sky shooting down on the city. Skyler and Nancy quickly jumped into the car. Skyler put up the hood of the car and drove, not caring about speed or the roads.

Skyler knew he had to get them out of there. Driving fast, there seemed no way to outrun the blasts. He had his gun next to him, but that was no match for the fighters. He could see Nancy trembling with fear she held on to her seat. *I got to get us back to base. But it's so far, I don't know what to do. Where can we go?* He couldn't leave the city. There was only one place in the city he knew they would be safe. "Hold on I have a plan and you will be safe."

Flooring it, he drove the car as fast as he could over anything small. In no time at all, he was at his uncle's house. The city was turning into a light show. Once past the gates he took Nancy's hand and ran with her into the house.

He couldn't hear anything inside the house. No bombs no shooting, the house was silent. Nancy looked around at the white walls with gold ivy covering embossed on them. The solid gold trim on the multiple round archways covering the windows. She looked up at the ceiling and saw lovely paintings of famous historical battles below her was a white marble floor. The hall on both sides seemed to go on forever.

She looked over at Skyler. "Where are we? Is this some kind of palace?"

Skyler was looking around wondering where the staff had all gone. "Ya, sort of, it doesn't have a big enough yard to be one or something my uncle is always complaining about that. But it is made to withstand most attacks."

Her eyes popped. "Wait did you say, uncle? Your uncle owns this place!"

Skyler rubbed his temples, the echoed in the building always bothered him. "Yes, this is my uncle's place he is out of town right now. He lets me come here anytime I want. Come on follow me I'll take you where you can relax."

Nearing the end of the seamlessly endless hallway they turned and went under one of the interior archways. This led to another hallway like the last but blue and gold decor. He kept going straight till they got to the billiard room.

The room was quite large big enough for person to live there. The room contained a modern leather sectional couch, flat holo screen TV, two holo pool tables, antique arcade machines, A bookshelf full games, a professional poker table, and fully stocked bar on the side of the room.

She turned to look at Skyler. "Wow, this place is amazing!"

Skyler grabbed the remote off the table and turned on the news. "Ya, it's pretty sweet, enjoy yourself sit down, there's a bar with everything you can enjoy. I have to make a few phone calls."

She walked to the bar and made herself a gin and tonic and sat down.

Skyler sat on the couch following the news. He got a hold of Michael. "Hey, they're bombing the city. What is it like over there?"

"I'm looking out the window now and nothing is here yet." He paused. "Wow, this attack is bad, I'm checking my tablet here now.

You're lucky you weren't killed, dude. I can drive Kax home tonight if that helps."

The news reporter announced on the screen. "The attacks have seemed to have stopped for now. The death toll is yet to be counted. But one death has been confirmed. Governor Styles was shot during the attack. The city mourns..."

Skyler's heart stopped when he saw who's face came on the news next.

The dark haired green skinned humanoid reporter turned to a man who Skyler knew all too well and wished he had been in that building when it was hit. The man being interviewed was no other than his stepfather Senator Charles Roux.

"I have now with me Senator Charles Roux. Now, sir, you were lucky to have survived the attack, where were you at the time?"

Charles Roux with his aging smile brushed back his dyed black thinning hair. He put on his slimy politician smile. "I was out to lunch with some other associates when we saw the attack across the street. My heart goes out to the victims and families of today's attack."

The reporter then asked. "Senator Roux why wasn't the Governor with your lunch party?"

"He had other matters to attend to." Charles put his head down. "With a heavy heart, I regret to say that he is no longer with us. But what I can say is that things are going to change. Things are going to get better and we are going to do whatever we can to stop this from happening again in the future."

"Skyler are you still there? I hear the TV, Skyler!" Michael called through the phone.

Skyler snapped back into reality. "The Cass got what they wanted. The governor is dead, give me some time I will be back at the academy to take Kax home." He hung up the phone without letting Michael finish.

Nancy walked over to Skyler handing him a drink. They both sat on the couch together. She placed her hand on his leg. "Do you want to talk about it?"

Skyler shook his head. He took a large sip of his drink before putting it down. She placed one hand on his face and kissed him seductively. He laid her down on the couch kissing her down her body. Undoing her top, he fondled her breasts unhooking her bra from the front. Sucking her breasts, he didn't want to think about the attack or his family he just wanted to be taken away to a place of sexual bliss. His communicator began to vibrate. "One moment." He groaned. He reached for his phone off the table and looked at the ID. "Shit, it's my mother." He dropped the phone on the coffee table and went back to Nancy. Ignoring the phone call as he fondled Nancy's body the phone went off again and again.

Fed up with the phone he finally picked up on the fifth call. "What do you want mother?" He hollered into the phone.

She snapped back. "Don't you speak to me that way! I was worried about you."

Skyler rolled his eyes. "Nice words to say to your son you haven't talked to in years. Mother, I saw the news. You can congratulate Charles for another competitor dying. I'm safe nothing hurt me, is that all?"

Taking a deep breath. "You have some mouth on you, you little brat is that what Leon is teaching you how to talk back to your mother."

Gripping the phone real tight. "Mother, I'm this close to smashing this communicator what did you call to talk to me about?"

"I'm glad you are safe. Your father and I want you to come to the governor's funeral with us. It would look good for the press and it has been a long time since we have all been together."

"The guy just died!" Rubbing his forehead. "No, I will not be there don't care, and Charles is not my father. Ask him why we haven't seen each other in so many years, don't blame me. Thanks a lot for calling when your husband is almost killed but not when your son was in the attack before. Very thoughtful of you." He hung up the phone and tossed it on the other side of the couch. Looking down at Nancy's exposed chest large perky breasts, he leaned down and continued where he left off.

"Are you sure you want to continue?" Nancy asked.

"Yes, it will help me calm down and clear my head." He kissed Nancy on the neck working his way down.

Returning to the academy, Nancy watched Skyler as he drove quietly back. "I guess you don't take too many girls to your uncle's place?"

Skyler shook his head. "Not anymore, when I was in high school and living here for a bit, I did. This was the first time since I joined the galactic forces that I have been back there. But I had to make sure you were safe. I'm sorry you had to deal with all of that."

She leaned over and gave him a kiss on the cheek. "It's alright, thank you for being my hero."

***

Kax looked at the time it was almost half an hour from the time she got off. She looked over at Michael who was waiting with her. "Just give me a ride I don't think he is coming. I want to go home."

Michael looked at his tablet to check to see if there were any messages from Skyler, "Look he said he would be here, and he will be here."

She was going to say another comment then she saw the electric green convertible pull up into the parking garage. She glared at Skyler when she saw Nancy was in the car with him.

Skyler got out of the car the same time Nancy did. "Sorry I'm late, the city is a bit of a mess right now."

Kax waited till Nancy had left before she ran over to Skyler giving him a big hug. "You might be a jerk sometimes, but I don't want you to die on me."

Confused he hugged her back. "You know I'm too stubborn to die."

Breaking the hug, she got into her seat of the car.

"I have got a couple of more things to do on base. I was just here waiting with Kax. You head home, I will see you at the cabin later." Michael waved to them making his way out of the parking garage.

Kax waited in the front seat of the car and waited as Skyler took his time in the trunk. "Hurry up, will you? What were you doing in the city anyway?"

Skyler closed the lid of the trunk and came around. He got in the car and handed her the six Catillion Lilies. "I was getting you these."

Her heart dropped, and her eyes began to water. She sniffed the purple and golden Catillion Lilies, then reached over and gave Skyler a big hug. "Is this why you were in the city? You risked your life for me, and you didn't get just any flowers, you got these ones. Oh, my Skyler you are just so wonderful."

"To be fair the attack happened after I got the flowers." He hugged her back. "They're sort of housewarming gift. I had planned to give them to you at the house. But I thought now was as good as any."

A tear came to her eyes. "Thank you, Skyler, they're wonderful."

"I care about you, Kax, and you're really special to me. I just want you to be happy." He placed his arm around her giving her half a hug.

Chapter 17

Skyler was still shaken up form the attack the day before, but without fail he was back in school going to class. He got to the classroom door to realize he was early, *I'm never early. I really must not have gotten sleep last night. Maybe I should go and see if Cane is around and talk to him.* He was about to walk away when O'Brien got to the classroom doors.

"Hey laddie what's up your almost never early?" O'Brien asked.

Skyler stopped walking towards Cane's office and turned to talk to O'Brien. "I guess I'm still shaken about the attack yesterday. I was in the city when it happened."

"Bloody, what were you doing there?" O'Brien unlocked the keys to the classroom. "Come in and let's talk about it."

Skyler followed him into the room. "I was out buying a gift for Kax when the attack happened, I waited it out at my uncles place."

"Damn lad, it's scary enough when it happens here on base but in public if you got killed it might be weeks before they found and identified your body." O'Brien put his bag on his desk.

I guess I never thought about that, Skyler sighed, "I guess that means you don't leave base much?"

O'Brien shook his head, "Rarely only when I need to visit my sons. Emily lives on base with her wife and I live off potatoes and they're available on base."

Skyler snorted, "I get it. Ya being so close to the attack was weird. I mean I really was on my own, and I was with Nancy so had to make sure she was okay. Why do you think the Cass are attacking us?"

O'Brien gave a shrug, "That I can't really answer, those Cassys are always fighting with us and think they are so powerful they can just come over here and blow the place up. They are warmongering bastards."

Skyler coughed, "Ugh is that the correct way to refer to them?"

O'Brien shook his index finger, "You're right old terms, let me correct myself. The Cass are warmongering bastards."

Skyler shrugged he didn't feel any better about the change, "Are they really all bad as you say?"

"With my experience yes, they are. Even the ones in the forces most of them are in David's fleet and they're quite bastards who are deadly. I wouldn't trust one even if they were raised on earth, they killed to many of my friends and have hurt so many more." O'Brien said with a deep sigh.

"So, what you are telling me is that they are heartless killers from another world who don't care about us?" Skyler asked.

O'Brien nodded, "Yup you can tell by their cold dark soulless eyes."

A Cassiopaean classmate entered the classroom and shot O'Brien a glare.

O'Brien leaned in and whispered to Skyler, "Did you see how it looked at me? I tell ya they're up to something."

Skyler awkwardly nodded his head, "Uh huh." He looked at the clock on the wall. "Sir, I think it's time to get ready for class."

O'Brien turned his head to look at the clock on the wall. He then looked towards the seats of the class and saw the room starting to fill. "I guess you're right Therris, go take a seat."

***

Later that night, Skyler put his clothes on and walked out of Nancy's room. Not caring who saw him he was not staying with Nancy. He felt worried and dirty for what he had done, this was not how he had expected his Friday night to have gone. He wasn't sure, but something didn't feel right. Nancy was getting out of hand. He went into that room hoping to have a good time with Nancy and her, Ray, but that is not what happened. Nancy mistreated them both in ways he was trying to wrap his head around.

Not sure where he was going, he just needed to clear his head. He walked through the empty grounds of the academy. It was nearing three in the morning too late to call Michael for a ride. Too late to call anyone. *Or was it*, He thought. He went down to the basement of the base. He knocked on the door.

Perry came to the door. "Hey buddy, what you are doing here?"

"Girl troubles. I don't have a place to go. Can I crash with you and your plants?"

Perry stepped aside letting Skyler in. "You can use my cot. I must continue working but I will be in the glass room in the back. If you need anything knock on the window. That's the room with the plants I'm on the diet for."

"Thanks, buddy," He dragged his feet over to the cot.

"You seem upset, not just tired, what happened?" Perry asked and walked over to Skyler.

"I didn't screw this one up, I'm dumping her. Having sex with her inexperienced girlfriend while she watched I was okay with, but to be forced to sleep with her after... If she would have given me the warning, I would have been fine. I used up all my energy on making Ray feel good, I didn't save any for Nancy. She should have respected that and not pinned me down and made me." Skyler got into the cot tossing a blanket over him.

"Dude that is messed up. Don't you think you should report her?" Perry asked.

"She hit me with a riding crop. I got marks all over my body. I really wish she would have given me a warning. That is not okay unless she asks first." He shook his head, "Why don't I report her? I would get in trouble for being in her room after hours. And then what we were doing is just not allowed."

"Yeah, I don't know what to say about that."

Skyler rolled onto his side and closed his eyes. "Were done. I'm just walking away from her. I would rather just never deal with her again."

"I don't blame you," Perry replied with a sad look on his face. "I'm sorry anything like that had to happen to you."

Chapter 18

Skyler was waiting for Kax to finish steaming his uniform. "Skyler you know that once you use this you get it cleaned and then leave it in the suit bag. You have had a lot of time to get this ready but now you make me steam at the last minute."

Walking over next to Kax in the laundry room. "You said you knew how to steam. I thought you were offering." Skyler watched her use the steamer on his forest green satin uniform.

She finished the pants and moved on to the jacket. "Well, at least you have your medals ready. Put the pants on and make sure they're okay. I don't like you walking around in just your boxers."

"Well would you prefer me to not wear anything at all? I really don't like the feeling of wearing pants all day." Skyler took the pants from her and tried them on. He checked the waist. "These pants seem a little big."

"I would prefer you to wear pants instead of boxers around the house." She stopped steaming and went over and checked Skyler's waist. "It seems like you have lost weight from the last time you wore these. There is no time to fix them you will have to wear your belt. You do have your dress belt still?"

Shaking his head. "They're optional so I never paid attention I might be able to find it somewhere in my stuff."

Clenching her fist. "You're so irresponsible, mister who wants to be a captain but can't even keep his track of his uniform."

Skyler laughed in amusement. "Well that's why I need a wife like you."

She lightly slapped his face. "And they say chauvinism is dead. I guess whoever said that never met you."

He rubbed his face still laughing. "Well is she hot? And do you have her number."

She tried not to laugh. "You're never going change, are you?"

"I'm teasing you." Putting on his sly smile, "But there is one girl I would change for."

She finished steaming his jacket. She handed it to Skyler. "Keep it clean and go see if you can borrow Michaels dress belt."

He took the jacket and put it on. Once he was all buttoned and zipped up he leaned in and gave Kax a kiss on the cheek. "Thank you, for putting up with me."

Kax blushed, before pushing him out of the room, "Go!"

Walking out of the room he went up the stairs to Michael's room. He knocked before he went in. "Hey, Michael I need to borrow a belt."

Michael was just finishing getting dressed. "What happened to your dress belt?"

Skyler shrugged sitting down on Michaels bed. "Well it's not mandatory, so I lost it. I think and well my pants don't fit me, so I thought I could borrow yours. I can't wear an everyday belt."

Michael walked over his closet and pulled out his extra dress belt. Sighing hesitantly, he turned around and handed the belt to Skyler. He and Skyler were both holding on to. "I want it back when you are done. No losing it."

Taking the belt. "No worries I just need it for the ceremony." He stood up and put it on, trying to get it to fit. "You Squallite's really are small this barely goes around me."

Looking at the belt, Michael checked the one he is wearing. "I guess I am just smaller sorry."

Finally getting it on. "Don't worry it will do the job, at least, I know you didn't take it."

Shooting Skyler, a glare, he was about to say something and when they heard Kax call up the stairs. "Come on guys it's time to go!"

At the main auditorium and they went down to the stage. Skyler hoped that Cane was there. He hadn't seen him in a few months and he was beginning to worry if he was ever coming back. With his well pressed green satin uniform and his medals on his left side. He sat down all ready to accept his award with the rest of the group. He looked there was, at least, Twenty, fold-out chairs ready for them. So, there was more than just his friends and Rob getting a medal today.

Skyler looked at the audience trying to see who was here. He saw Michael's and Kax's father but not his mother. He didn't pay any attention to the date. He thought, *Maybe she is at the governor's funeral that's all.* He wasn't going to show that it upset him, his mother wasn't there she didn't come to any of his other events. He spotted O'Brien in the crowd. *He must be here for me.* It didn't matter if his mother was there or not, he chose the path that was right for him. His friends supported him. Waiting for the ceremony to start he saw Cane at the side of the stage. It brought joy to him to see Cane again and well. He knew that Cane had to be there to give medals to his fleet but even if he didn't have to Cane would have been there for him.

The ceremony was long. The names were called in alphabetical order. Skyler and Kax were near the end, but they did eventually get their service medals and bravery medals. Skyler wanted to give Cane a big hug when he saw him. He was so happy to see a comforting familiar face.

After the ceremony, Skyler separated from the group giving time to Kax and Michael to be with their families while he went looking for his, Cane. Walking around he couldn't find him. While searching O'Brien tapped him on the shoulder. "Congratulations Laddie."

Skyler turned around and smiled. "Thank you, sir."

O'Brien gave Skyler a hug. "You're a brave kid, I'm happy that you are safe. I just thought I would let you know I have written up your letter of recommendation for the command program on Tauron for you like you requested. I feel you will do great in their program."

Skyler sighed. "Thank you, sir, but I have thought it over and I feel I would do better if I did my command training on Catillion."

O'Brien raised an eyebrow. "Now Lad that is a different ball game. Are you sure? This isn't just about Kax is it?"

Skyler shook his head. "I have given it some thought, and I think it might be a better career move. It's also a bigger base. It's a major one like Earth, I think. I will fit in better."

"You realize that Tauron is a command base. Its focus is training future captains and admirals. Fleet Admiral Davis was trained on Tauron."

Skyler nodded. "Exactly. I have investigated the records of the officers who did their training on Tauron. Great powerful officers but very strict and militaristic. I know I might not be the most obedient cadet. But I think getting an education on a base in another Galaxy from another race with a different ideology would benefit me more."

O'Brien was silent for a moment, then he let out a loud roar and patted Skyler on the back. "Now that is called using your head Lad, I like it. I'll write you a great letter. You will go in there a kitten and come out a lion. I have got to go now, Laddie. I will see you in class tomorrow and congratulations on that medal."

Skyler smiled checking out his new medal pinned to his chest with the others. "Thank you, sir, I will see you then." He waved goodbye to O'Brien. He turned around and saw Rey standing behind him. "Oh hello, how are you doing?"

She looked down at her feet, "I'm sorry for what Nancy did to you. She has done the same to me and well I think you can tell."

He put his hand on her shoulder. "I thought there was something up with you on Friday I just couldn't say anything. Are you okay?"

Rey shook her head. "At first yes, I was used to that kind of behavior. People have always been rough with me. But when I was with you, I realized that there are nice people. I noticed a big difference. You respected me."

Skyler's ego when up about ten points and he gave a sympatric smile. "Well I do try. Are you still with Nancy?"

She shook her head. "I haven't told yet, I saw her on Sunday, but that was the end. Being with her was not the same after I had been with you. I saw what she did to you and realized what she had done to me."

Skyler gave her a hug. "I'm not talking to her anymore." Not wanting to think about Nancy and the horrible things she had done to him. "My business with her is done and that is it."

"Is it possible, maybe we could go on a date together?" She asked slowly while clenching her fists and twisting her foot.

He let out a deep sigh. "I don't date, and with our connection with Nancy I wouldn't recommend it right now." He saw the sadness in her eye. *This girl really needs someone to be kind to her.*

"Okay." She said sadly.

"I do know a guy who would be interested, if you're looking for another relationship. No offense I'm just not the dating type. But this guy he will treat you with respect and show you how to have fun without having sex. I think you two will get along if you're okay with that, I could ask him?" He asked her.

She hugged him back tightly and blushed. "You're a sweet guy I'll send you my number later. Nancy gave me yours. Thank you." She broke the hug and walked away.

He waved goodbye to her.

Kax tapped him on the shoulder. "Hey Skyler, I was wondering if you were coming home tonight?"

Huh? I didn't think about that. He was not sure what to say. "I didn't have any plans I don't have to if you don't want me to?"

Shaking her head. "No, it is alright. It was just that Michael is going to stay the night at his dad's place and my dad wants to come over and I thought about giving him your room or Michael's and I just wanted to know what your plans were?"

Cane who was now standing behind Skyler put his hand on the boy's shoulder, "He does have plans, so you can do whatever you like my dear."

He jumped when he felt the hand on his shoulder, swiftly turning around. "Cane? I do have plans?"

Cane nodded his head. "Yes, you do and they're with me."

Skyler looked back at Kax shrugging. "Well Kax I will see you in class tomorrow then and have a good night."

Smiling at Skyler, she left the auditorium to go do what she wanted.

Cane gave Skyler a hug. "Come on I have something to show you." Cane walked out of the room and walked with Skyler to the main base of the grounds.

Following him, Skyler was wondering why they were going over here. "Uh, sir why are we leaving the academy part and going to the actual base?"

Cane walked next to Skyler. "Because I think it's time, we go to this place together." Taking him past the barracks and parade square, they reached the main hall.

Skyler had only been in this building a few times. It was where they held fancy banquets, funerals and other formal gathering on base. Looking at the twenty-foot ceiling, the walls were a sea foam and green turquoise with white pillars around the hall for decoration. They walked on the stone floor. He had only ever been to the main room at the end of the long hallway. He did not know where Cane was leading him. He followed Cane past the main hall almost the back of the building and then he went down a solid oak spiral staircase. Then entered a room that seemed plain and boring compared to the rest. Small beige walls and gray carpet with just a basic wooden desk. *Where are we going?* No one was sitting at the desk. Cane pulled out his key card and scanned it on the decorative glass doors behind the desk.

"Come on follow me it's not much further," Cane said holding the door open for Skyler.

Tired and nervous Skyler followed Cane once again. When they walked through the glass door the it was like he was in another world. The room had nicely polished white and blue marble floor that reflected off the ceiling that was painted in to match the night sky, it was a galaxy of rainbow gasses and bright stars. It was what was on the walls that sent chills down Skyler's spine. He was unsure why Cane had brought him to a place like this, but he knew deep in his gut it was important. They were like glass show cases ranging from 1-2 square feet. They were sealed in by the glass and illuminated by bright lights. Each had its own spot some had former possessions around them, others were barren. *Urn's, they are holding urns.* Skyler walked up to one on that caught his eye on the wall. A Jade green metal urn that read Cartwright. There was a small black metal plaque behind it that had a blurb of the story of the late Admiral Cartwright who had died fighting in the first Space War. In front of the plaque was his medals.

Turning to look at Cane who was making his way further down the hallway. Skyler's hands were trembling, and his heart was racing. "Why did you bring me to a place like this? Cane explain to me what you are doing."

Cane turned around and let out a sigh. "It's called a Columbarium and come here, there is someone here you need to see."

His chest tightened, and his knees became weak. *Who's here? Why would they be here?* These questions raced through his mind.

Finally, Cane stopped. He went to a large red and gold urn. to the side. there was a plaque and in front of it were the medals and a couple of photos. Cane didn't need to say anything. Skyler saw the name on the urn and he knew why he was here. He finally knew why this was so important. He recognized the man in the three photos. It was his father's urn.

Reading the name Therris over again in his mind he fell to his knees. He looked at the three photos. There was his Fathers graduation photo, another his wedding photo and the third was a picture of him holding a young Skyler. Trying to hold back the tears, there was a sharp pain in his chest. He grasped his chest, thinking of something to say. "I was told my father didn't have a grave."

Cane's jaw dropped when he heard Skyler's words. "Of course, he does, who told you he didn't?"

Skyler tears ran down his eyes. "My mother always told me my father went down with his ship and his body was destroyed and he is now space dust."

A disgusted look crossed his face, Cane knelt putting his arm around Skyler. "That's how he died, but just as the ship was destroyed, we were able to transport the body out of there, what was left of it. It wasn't pretty, but we got him out. I don't understand why your mother never told you about this. I'm so sorry, I thought you knew."

Skyler cried into his hands. "I wish I would have known. My dad has been this close all these years. I thought there was nothing."

Cane pulled out his key card, handing it to Skyler. "Here you have permission to come here anytime you want. I brought you here today because a long time ago I promised your dad if his son ever got a medal of bravery that I would make sure he would see it. I'm also supposed to do a few other things for him, but that's all to come. I would have taken you here sooner if I would have known."

Wiping the tears away he took the black key card. "Thank you, Sir, you don't know what this means to me."

"I have a pretty good idea." Cane sat down next to Skyler looking up at the tomb he took a deep breath. "I come here quite a bit, I came here when you joined the academy to tell your father that you were a cadet. Told him when you got your first medal when you finished your first year, when you went away. I tell him everything I can about you. Not sure if or where his soul is. Or if he can hear, but this is as close as I'm going to get. I have been coming here a lot lately so many things have happened, and this is one of the places I like to come and think. These walls are filled with people I have worked with. Not all of them but many."

He picked his head up and looked at Cane, he sniffled. "Is Kax's mom here too?"

Cane shook his head. "No, her family took her body back, not sure where it is, they had the memorial here. The funeral was private for the family."

Looking back on his father's two-foot wide tomb and noticed an empty one next to it, "Why is my dad's tomb so big and who's the empty one for."

Letting out a big sign. "Your mother was supposed to be next to him, but I don't know what her plans are now. She is still an officer. She is entitled to a spot here. But not sure what she will pick. She went back to her maiden name as soon as your dad died. She didn't want to keep it. You're lucky she didn't succeed in changing your name. The one next to his is Mine. It is a bit smaller, but I don't think I will have anyone else in there with me so."

"She did try to change my name when she married Charles. I refused." Looking at all the other urns on the wall. "Do I have a spot?"

Cane raised an eyebrow. "Do you want one? I can get you one. All officers are entitled to one but not all take it. You still must pay for them, they're not free. Not just anyone can be entombed here. Some choose to go home to their families and there are other ones like this on other planets. People might choose to be there. Some get shot off into space. If you really want one, I will get you one."

Skyler gave a faint smile. "I might love the stars, but I think I want to spend the afterlife with my father."

Cane stood up. He walked to the end of the hall to a small office. Stepping in he walked into the five by six office and typed a few things into the computer on the desk.

Skyler followed right behind him.

"There is nothing in your dad's section but they're building a new section. If you want your dad's spot you will have to ask your mother for permission her name is still on the box. If not, I can get you room in another section?"

"I'll think about talking to my mother about it. If not how much farther is this section?" Skyler asked looking at the wall.

Cane gave a little laugh. "Like your dad thinking ahead. I was with him when he bought his, we came back from our first dangerous mission and he said, 'I need to make plans in case I don't come back.' He picked that spot because the constellation above him is Orion and that is where he almost died the first time, he wanted it to be a memory. The closest I can get you is in the Perseus section it is a double unit and you're about four sections away from your dad. But I can put you on a waitlist in case someone changes their mind later. Not everyone who owns these has passed yet, and from time to time they do get refunded."

Skyler nodded. "Perseus is just fine, all sounds good. So, you run this department too?"

Cane shook his head. "No, I just have access to all the files because of my rank. I can't change anything just add in new stuff."

Skyler pulled out his wallet. "How much do I owe you for it?"

"Put your money away. Consider it an early graduation gift. Your father wouldn't want me to charge you for something like this. Now the rest of your funeral you plan for yourself. I will be long gone before that day comes."

"Thank you, Leon."

Chapter 19

Waking in a strange bed, Skyler tried to recollect his memories from last night. The last thing he remembered he was at a bar with Cane. He quickly looked around the room trying to see if there were any clues. His dress uniform folded and placed on a chair and hanging off the back of the chair was a fresh set of clothes, that were not any he recognized. With a hangover he got up out of the twin bed, hardwood floors a desk with powder blue walls. *This is Cane's house.*

After putting on the blue T-shirt and worn out blue jeans, he walked down to the hall trying to find someone else in the house. The room he was in was about eighteen by twenty it seemed small compared to the rest of the house. Walking around on the unfamiliar light hardwood flooring. He called down from the railing of the white painted spiral staircase. "Cane are you there?"

Cane came to the stairs. "Good you're up I will drive you back to your house if that's okay?"

Skyler walked down the stairs holding onto the railing. "Don't I have to go to the academy today?"

Cane shook his head. "I run it, you don't have to go if I say you don't plus it is 2PM you have missed most of the day and you don't have your cadet uniform."

Rubbing his face and walking towards the kitchen that. He could see behind Cane the stairs. "Okay then who's clothes are these and how did I get my uniform off?"

Cane followed him to the kitchen pouring him and Skyler both a cup of coffee. "After the columbarium, we went to the bar to celebrate. You had way too many drinks and I called my driver to pick us up. Once we got back, I helped you take your clothes off. You don't want to get your dress uniform wrinkled. And helped you to bed. I didn't have nearly as many drinks as you did." He turned and walked over to the kitchen table and handed Skyler his drink. "The clothes you're wearing are mine, my old clothes. I don't fit them anymore. I knew you would need clothes, so I went looking before I fell asleep. That's why they're worn out, it's got to be at least twenty years since I last wore them. I'm glad they fit you."

Drinking his coffee, he looked at the old worn faded jeans and smiled. "Thanks, Cane for everything, you're awesome."

Cane smiled like a father watching his own son. "Leon. You don't always have to call me Cane. I told you once before you could call me Blinky, your dad gave me that nickname. But if you don't feel right you can just call me Leon."

Skyler looked down into his coffee mug. "Whatever you say, Leon. So, you live alone why do you have such a big house?"

Cane shook his head. "I don't know. I know certain things I need to have room for, like the big dining room and a nice backyard for when to have parties and such but the rest I'm not sure about. I wish I had someone here, but I have always been alone. They expect Fleet Admirals to have these big homes for parties and meetings. I have a maid who lives here some of the time."

Sighing Skyler took another sip of his coffee.

Leon finished up his cup. "Come on finish up that cup and I will drive you home."

Skyler took the last sip of his coffee. Then went upstairs and got his uniform. He made his way back down.

Cane handed him a suit bag and a medal case. "Put your uniform in this so it doesn't get ruined and keep your medals in this case. You're going to need to get them mounted now that you have so many."

Skyler placed his uniform in the bag once he was done. "So, were you really on Lyra City for the last few months?"

Shaking his head. "Officially yes, the real answer I was on Capella. I had a warning of an assignation attempt on my life, so I said I went to Lyra City on vacation, but really I was hiding on Capella."

Skyler zipped up the bag. "Why Capella isn't that a farming planet?"

Leon laughed. "It's more than just that but my job on the planet was just taking care of some old things and no one would expect me there. But that is a story for another day, let's get going."

***

The house was empty. Skyler walked through the door. He looked for a note or something. Looking at the clock, he knew Kax and Michael would be home soon. Noticing Cane was standing at the door. He turned and said. "You can come in if you want to?"

Cane shook his head. "No not today. This place has too many memories for me right now. Maybe next time I will come in. I hope you have a good time and see you in school tomorrow."

Skyler put his stuff down, went back to the door and hugged Cane. "Thank you for everything Leon."

Holding back his tears he hugged Skyler back. "Anytime Skyler."

Once Cane was gone Skyler went to his bedroom to put his uniform in the closet. He noticed that the bed had not been touched. *I guess David stayed in Michael's room?* Once his uniform was away, he stoped by Michael's room to return the belt. *Michael's bed is perfect too.* The room was left the way Michael leaves, it with the blankets pulled tighter than they should and not a wrinkle in sight. *This is odd,* He thought. *It's almost like no one came over last night. Maybe he stayed in the basement?*

He walked into Kax's room just to see what her bed looked like. It was messed up. She didn't even make the effort to make it. He was shocked to see how messy it was. Not that he had seen how she slept often, just it wasn't like anything he has seen before. Stepping into her room to get a closer look. He heard a crunch under his foot. His eyes widened, and a huge smile came over his face. He bent over and picked up a condom wrapper. *Right,* He knew then her dad didn't stay over, she had a guy over. He left the room and went down to the couch and sat there with the wrapper in hand. He was not going to let Kax get away this that easy.

Within the hour, Kax came in the door. Skyler turned around to face her. "So how was your night? Which room did you dad sleep in?"

She stopped at the door and looked at Skyler. "What do you mean?"

Skyler held up the condom wrapper. "I'm going to take a guess your dad didn't sleep over."

She sighed and sat down next to Skyler on the couch. "No, he didn't, we had dinner together and then he went home. I decided to take your advice and have a one-night stand."

His eyes were wide with shock. "I'm impressed. I'm glad you got laid, but I never said have a one-night stand. I always say you should get laid, not how, and preferably with me."

She covered her face. "It was a big mistake okay Skyler. I had a moment of weakness and just took him here for sex. I feel dumb and stupid."

Skyler put his arm around Kax. "You're not stupid, you used a condom."

She leaned against Skyler almost like giving him a hug without the arms. "It was fun. I had fun. He had fun, but why do I feel so dirty? How do you do it?"

He tried not to laugh. "The more you do it the less dirty and the easier it gets. But next time you get the urge to have random sex ask me first."

Michael walked in the door just in time to hear the last line Skyler said. "Do I want to know what is going on?"

Skyler moved Kax off him and stands up. "No, you don't, but I got you a girlfriend."

He rolled his eyes and walked up the stairs to his room.

Skyler got off the couch and followed Michael. "Listen, buddy, I know you don't want to have sex and you have your own thing going on, but she is not that kind of girl. Remember that girl I was seeing, Nancy? Well Nancy and her girlfriend Rey broke up and Rey is looking for a boyfriend. One who won't use her. I don't know her whole story, but she has been used and abused too many times. She's eighteen and I thought you would be perfect. Your harmless when it comes to women and thought if you went on one or two dates just to show her there're nice guys out there. Please, just do me this favor?"

Michael turned around and glared at Skyler. "I am not sure what part I should hit you for. The part where you volunteered me for going on a blind date without asking me. The part that you never listen to me. Or that you think your word is law and that I will listen to you no matter what you say?"

Shaking his head Skyler let out a deep sigh. "Fine, don't go out with her. Don't listen to me and try something new. I didn't say sleep with her. That's the opposite of what she needs right now. I wouldn't have picked you if I didn't think you were a decent guy, okay, I'm sorry." He turned and walked out of the room.

Michael shouted so Skyler could hear him. "Fine, I will go on one date that is it!"

Skyler smirked as he walked back downstairs.

Chapter 20

"What are you doing?"

Michael looked over his shoulder and saw Rob standing over him. "I am working that is what. Why do you always stand over me?"

"I enjoy watching you work." Rob said with a sly grin and pulled a chair up beside Michael. "So, what's new with you?"

Michael sighed. "I do not mind being friends, but I do not like sharing my work with anyone. Can I please work in peace?"

"Then why are you working on a project with Perry Zyrix?" Rob asked.

"How do you know that?" Michael raised an eyebrow.

"Well one I know you're friends with him and two I work with the greenhouse too. It is my job to find ingredients and supplies. Why did you think I was in this class?" Rob mentioned. "My expertise is finding new sources for chemicals and ways to concentrate them better. I'm training to be a captain of a science ship. What did you think I was doing here?"

Michael froze he never thought much of Rob. "I never really thought about it. I am sorry about being so rude."

Rob shook his head. "Don't you worry about it. You were protecting your research. Which is something we all should do. But Perry has informed me you're having problems finding large sources of a few starter ingredients for the next batch of plants. I was wondering if we could combine our heads and see what we could do to find them?"

Michael slid his notebook over Rob. "I need to find almost a liter of these chemicals. But if I order from any lab, they will give me milliliters It takes too long and costs a lot of money to get this much of one chemical. Let alone all five of them. I have been trying to find a way, but we need this for the starter."

Rob was silent for a moment as he read over the notes. "Aren't high amounts of these chemicals found commonly in decaying Squallite and Catillion bodies? And a few other species?"

"Yes, but Squallites do not donate their bodies to science in anyway. Catillions are very picky about their burial rituals. So, I have no choice but to get them from plant sources. And plants produce very little." Michael explained.

"Now is this for every plant or just the starter?" Rob asked.

"Starter to create and breed them. Once the plant grows, we should be able to reproduce it without this starter." Michael stated.

"I will get you what you need," Rob closed the books and stood up.

"Do not kill anyone." Michael stared at Rob with worried eyes.

"No one will die specifically for this project. But it's lunchtime are you coming?" Rob got up and took his bag.

"No, I packed my lunch today. I want to get as much work as I can get done." Michael replied.

"Well then I will see you later." Rob made his way out of the room.

***

Skyler looked up from his lunch. He saw Rob standing on the other side of the table with his tray in hand.

"Hey Skyler, long time no see. How are the ladies treating you?" Rob said to him.

Skyler rolled his eyes. "No offense but I don't want to talk about my love life with anyone right now."

Rob took his seat. "Nancy not treating you right?"

113

Skyler groaned not wanting to think about that night. "Me and Nancy are over. I would prefer never to deal with her again but I'm helping out her other ex, right now."

"That bad huh, well I'm sorry she did that to you," Rob said trying to sound sympathetic.

Skyler dropped his fork. "What do you know about what Nancy did to me? How do you seem to always know what is going on when no one has told you anything? Are you spying on us?"

"You're just easy to read." Rob took a bite of his salad and replied calmly. "You think by not saying anything you are not telling me something? You and most people wear your emotions on your face. It's not hard to figure out that you were abused by Nancy. I also used to date her."

Skyler shot Rob a glare and swiped his hand through the air in a horizontal cutting action. "Shut your mouth now!"

"I over spoke, I will drop the subject." Rob continued with his salad.

Kax came over with her tray. Today she just had a pudding cup and gelatin on her tray. "Hey guys, what's up?"

"Rob's attitude." Skyler snarled.

Kax looked at the silent Rob. "So, no Michael?" She took a seat next to Skyler.

"Michael decided to work through lunch." Rob's eyes pointed to Kax's tray. "On a diet or something?"

She bit her lip and shook her head. "No, my stomach isn't feeling well so I want to keep my diet light."

"I would recommend drinking lots of orange tree tea. I think it will help you a lot at this time." Rob mentioned.

Kax shot Rob a glare. She leaned over and whispered to Skyler. "You're right."

Skyler raised an eyebrow in confusion. *What's wrong with a tea suggestion?*

"You do know I'm a command scientist, right? That suggestion didn't come out of nowhere." Rob pointed out.

"Rob, could you try to talk about the non-awkward subjects today?" Skyler asked.

Rob finished his bite of salad. "When do you think the next attack will be?"

Skyler let out a sigh in defeat. *I miss Michael.*

Chapter 21

Michael was combing his hair when Skyler entered the room.

"Dude the girl is not going to care if your hair is parted perfectly or not." Skyler mockingly joked with Michael.

Putting his comb down he turned and glared at Skyler. "I have never been on a real date with someone I do not know. I want to make sure I do this right."

Sitting down on Michael's bed he watched him get ready. "So where are you two going?"

Michael changed out of a t-shirt and put on an orange dress shirt. "Dinner, there is a nice whole food restaurant I know, and I figured I would take her there."

"Wait a moment. She's a Catillion you can't feed her salad they need to eat meat."

Doing up the last button on his shirt. "You still eat meat, on the whole food diet, just real meat not replicated."

"Really, but I always see you eat salad and fruit?"

Groaning Michael ignored Skyler's comment. "You are sitting on my tie."

Skyler shifted pulling the tie from under his butt. "Sorry dude." He handed him the tie, "Here you go."

Michael let out a big sigh. "Skyler is it okay if I borrow your car for the night?"

Pulling out the keys of his pocket, "Sure, no problem but if you do decide to get a little freaky don't do it in the car. That's only for me to do."

Hesitantly, Michael took the keys. "Do I need to wash the seats first?"

While laughing, he got off the bed. "No, they're leather everything just wipes off."

Skyler left the room and walked down the stairs. He went and sat next to Kax on the couch. "So, Michael is going out for the night what do you want to do?"

Staring at the smirk on Skyler's face, she rolled her eyes. "Not the same thing you want to do. I was just going to have a quiet night, but you don't know what that word means."

His smirk got bigger. "Well, to be fair, I'm the quiet one it's the girls that make all the noise."

Shifting on the couch away from him. "Skyler, I have been sick for the last week, sex is the last thing on my mind."

Frowning in worry. "Sick like how? I haven't seen you sneezing or coughing."

Covering her face. "I have been throwing up constantly and food tastes so icky to me. I hate this." Holding on to her stomach. "Just nauseous, all day and night. I have been trying to get over it, but nothing works."

"Kax, I think we need to go the doctor and get you checked out. It's only been about two weeks since you had sex unless there was someone before?" Skyler looked at her with suspicion. "Are you nauseous right now? Do you have a fever, do your breasts hurt? Any other symptoms?"

Turning to glare a Skyler. "What does my sex life have to do with me being sick?" She paused for a second, then her jaw dropped. "You think I'm pregnant, don't you?"

116

"I have been around pregnant women before." He paused waiting for her reaction, "Well, what else could it be?"

"The stomach flu, you idiot!" She got up and ran to the bathroom.

Skyler followed her to the bathroom. "But you don't have fevers or other symptoms, and this happened after your one-night stand."

"We used a condom remember?" She paused then threw up into the toilet. "Fine. I will take a dumb test, but you have to take me to the doctor since it is all your idea."

Skyler helped hold her hair back. "If you are, what are you going to do about it?"

She finished up and sat on the floor. "I'm not pregnant, I'm just sick! I can't be pregnant." She finished throwing up, "Just leave me alone Skyler."

Skyler left the bathroom and rushed to the living room to try and catch Michael before he left.

Michael had just finished putting on his jacket.

"Michael you can't take the car tonight. Kax isn't well and I need to take her to the doctor." He said panting.

"You promised me the car," Michael let out a sigh. "But if Kax needs a doctor I guess you could go with her." Michael pulled the keys out of his pocket. "Why do you just call Dr. Kelley maybe he will stop by?"

Skyler thought about it for a second. "I guess I could see, she's not that sick I could always take her tomorrow. You know what, take the car and pick up Rey, you've never been on a date that's more important, Kax can wait."

"If she gets worse call me," Michael said as he walked out the door.

Skyler rushed over to the coffee table and picked up his communicator and called Dr. Kelley's after-hours number. "Hey doc, Kax is sick and she might be pregnant, could you come out here or do we have to go see you tomorrow?"

Skyler could hear Dr. Kelley type in a few things. "I'm leaving town tomorrow. This is Skyler, right? I can stop by and see how Kax is doing. Are you still on base?"

"No, we moved off base, but I will send you the address. Thanks, doc see you in a bit." He hung up the phone and went back to the bathroom where Kax was just getting ready to leave. "Good news Kax, Michael is gone, and Dr. Kelley is on his way over to check you out. He is leaving town so that's why is stopping by."

Kax snapped at Skyler. "You did what? I told you I'm not pregnant, why did you call the doctor?"

He went to put his hand on her shoulder. "Listen to me Kax, I have been around pregnant women before, and I think you just might be. If not see him anyways as he might have something to cure your stomach flu."

She pushed his hand out of the way and went and sat on the couch. She began to cry, "I don't want to be pregnant not like this, it's all your fault! What do you know about pregnant women, you probably knocked one up! Do you have a kid running around that you haven't told me about?"

"I better not have a kid." Skyler's heart stopped for a second. "I don't have a kid. But one of my high school girlfriends was pregnant. I was in a triad with my friend Paul and our girlfriend got pregnant. We didn't know who the father was for months. Finally, we were able to get a test and it was a big relief when it was his."

A disgusted look came over her face. "You continued to sleep with her?"

"She was both our girlfriend." Walking over he sat next to Kax. "It wasn't mine and she couldn't get pregnant twice. What's the harm? But don't worry I always use condoms, I don't have any kids running around." A smirk crossed his face, "Unless you want me to be the father to your baby?"

Rubbing her head. "I'm not pregnant okay. I'm just sick!" She sat with Skyler on the couch quietly waiting for the doctor.

He had a deep sinking feeling that Kax wasn't telling him the whole story. *Kax why don't you trust me to tell me the truth?*

"Skyler what if I really am pregnant? What do I tell my Dad? What will I do about the forces? Who would raise the baby? I don't want to have a baby, not now during a war." The tears were rolling down her face.

Skyler held her close. "We will figure this out. I will be there for you. Even if we're just friends, I will help you take care of this baby." He closed his eyes. *Shit, I don't want a kid. I don't want kids. But Kax has more to lose than me. I may not want it, but I must do the right thing.*

Skyler held Kax close until there was a knock at the door. Skyler jumped off the couch to let the doctor in. "Thank you for coming. Kax is sitting on the couch."

The doctor went over to the couch and sat down. He put his doctor's bag on the coffee table and pulled out his stethoscope, tongue depressor, and flashlight. He looked at Kax. "So, what are your symptoms?"

She had sadness still in her eyes. "I'm moody, I have been throwing up day and night and besides that nothing. Skyler thinks I'm pregnant."

"Well then the question is are you sexually active?" Dr. Kelley pressed his stethoscope to her chest. "Breathe for me. Normally I would say you couldn't have morning sickness this early, but you're a Catillion so you can have it at almost any time because your pregnancies are a lot shorter than humans. I think you only have one for twenty-four weeks, not forty weeks which human women have. Breathe for me."

"I have had sex twice in the last month." She took a deep breath in and out as he moved the stethoscope around her chest. She watched as he put it down and used the tongue depressor and checked her throat for anything odd.

Twice? Skyler's eyes widened. "When was the other time?"

She gripped onto the pillow next to her on the couch. "I'll tell you about it later."

"You don't have the flu, but it could still be something else." He reached into his bag and pulled out a cup. "Pee in this and I will test the urine."

Nervous and worried she took the cup in her shaking hand and went to the bathroom.

Skyler turned to Dr. Kelley. "Thanks for coming, this really means a lot to me. I didn't think you made house calls."

Dr. Kelley smiled. "I owe you a lot and I'm going away for a few months tomorrow and thought I would use this to thank you and say goodbye for a bit. So, are you the father or is it someone else?"

Skyler shook his head. "No, we're just friends, besides she wouldn't let me get past first base and were not together she told me she picked up some random guy. I'm willing to help her raise the baby if she is, though, if she will have me. What are our options?"

"Read this." Dr. Kelley pulled a pamphlet out of his bag and handed it to Skyler. "You're a good kid I hope for you two she's not. But not many men would be willing to do what you're doing."

Skyler sighed. "I have been here before. I know she needs someone by her side. I'm not going to turn my back on her."

Kax came out of the bathroom a few minutes later with the cup of urine in her hand. "I hope this is all you need."

He took the cup from her and put a little test strip in. They all watched the strip change color to a bright pink. He looked up at Kax. "For a Catillion that means pregnant."

She sat back down on the couch and started to cry. "No this can't happen. I'm a pilot, I can't be pregnant. What do I do?"

Dr. Kelly started to pack up his bags. "Well this may be wrong, I can't confirm anything till you have an ultrasound. There are a few other doctors on base that are qualified Catillion doctors, but you still must wait for that baby to get bigger. Being a Catillion you have a few uteri that block each other, once one expands we can't tell by Earth ultrasound. I don't think we have a Catillion ultrasound on Earth base. What species was the guy?"

She hesitated. "Squallite."

Skyler's eyes popped. *Michael? Naw. Rantra? I sure hope not.*

Dr. Kelley nodded. "That could be why you are getting symptoms so early. Squallite babies are huge compared to Catillion and most human babies." He pulled out his tablet. "I can get you in for an appointment at the beginning of January. I want you to see a specialist on cross-species pregnancies. There is a chance a Squallite baby might be too big for you."

She held her stomach and her eyes were wide with worry. "What does that mean? What does this mean for my piloting career? What do I do for the next month and a half?"

"Until your appointment, you are to be treated like your pregnant. As for being a pilot talk to your instructor about that. I'm not a gynecologist and not an expert in cross-species biology and only know the basics in Catillion biology. So, I don't know, that's why I'm sending you to the specialist."

Kax put her head down with tears forming in her eyes. "Thank you for your help."

Dr. Kelley packed up his bag. "I wish you the best of luck. I must be off." He got up and waved goodbye to the two.

Skyler looked at Kax with all seriousness and without thinking he blurted out, "I will marry you and raise that baby with you if you want. But you got to tell me who the father is? It doesn't seem like a casual thing anymore."

Her tears got heavier. "I will tell you, but you can't tell anyone not even Michael. He can know about the baby but not the father."

Skyler frowned. "What are you trying to say?"

"Remember last year when I became friends with Jake and Ron?" She let out a sigh. "Ron is in the hospital and dying. Jake was upset. The first time we didn't use a condom but the second time we did. I can't tell Jake because he would not want this, and it would be proof we betrayed Ron."

Skyler rubbed his face. "Wait. I thought you told me he liked men and wasn't interested in you?"

"Jake is bisexual. He wasn't interested in me. But it was more of a bonding moment. We connected based on our history with each other." She grabbed the box of tissues off the coffee table.

Skyler nodded his head. "Okay, I can deal with this. I'll keep your secret and stay by your side." He took her hand. "You got me. You won't have to do this alone."

"Thank you, Skyler." She gave him a smile. They sat and held each other for a while.

CRASH! Michael burst through the front door out of breath he grabbed the remote and turned on the TV. Rey came running in after him. Michael saw Kax asleep in Skyler's arms on the couch. He quickly woke them up so he could sit on the couch and turned on the TV.

The reporter on the TV stood in front of United Galactic Forces base engulfed in flames. "Just now a major attack on the United Galactic Forces base. A large battleship came down from the sky and landed next to the main hall of the base sending units into the building. While other smaller Cassiopaean fighters flew around the city firing shots around the city. Death counts are not in yet but one death we are all certain of." The reporter stopped to listen to the message in their earpiece, "This just in, Fleet Admiral Thompson is dead, the units we saw from the main ship went into the building and found him. Cameras did catch the footage but due to its disturbing nature, we are not allowed to show it. What I can tell you is he was dragged out of his office by one of the Cassiopaean's to the top of the main hall and beheaded. This is a sad day for all. The battleship appears to have left now, but the damage is horrendous!"

They all watched the news in horror. Skyler looked over at Michael. "So how did you get here so fast?"

Rey spoke up. "I had just finished getting ready when Michael showed up. I got in the car when the battleship came and started shooting. Michael turned the car around and sped off in this direction."

A little shell-shocked Skyler's eyes widened. "Wow, that is amazing how you made it out. Perfect timing."

Kax sat down in shock. "Dr. Kelley was here during the attack, we saved his life. If he wasn't here…"

Skyler holding Kax closer, comforting her. "I guess you're right. Now calm down Kax it will all be okay." He felt her body trembling in his arms.

Michael looked at Kax. "So, what did the doctor say, are you okay?"

She didn't want to say anything in front of Rey, but she couldn't think of anything else to say but the truth. "He thinks I'm pregnant. But he is sending me to a specialist to make sure."

Rey sat next to Skyler. "Congratulation you two. Don't worry me and Skyler only had sex once and it won't happen again he's all yours."

Kax's eyes widen. She snapped. "It's not Skyler's. I have never slept with him and I don't plan to!"

Rey shifted back. "Oh, I'm sorry I just-"

Skyler cut her off. "Kax is tired and isn't well. I'm going to put her to bed. I'll come back and join you two." Skyler got off the couch with Kax and helped her up the stairs.

**

Michael looked at Rey. "Sorry date night is canceled, I know this is not really my place, but I do not think anyone is going to argue with it. You can stay till this all blows over and the streets are safe. There is a spare room in the basement if you want or you can have the couch."

Rey smiled. "You're a sweet guy Michael and thank you for saving my life."

Michael hadn't thought of it like that. In a way, he had saved her life. Who knows what would have happened to her if he arrived a moment later. The base was all under attack it was a light show. Not a major attack they knew what they wanted, and they came and got in. Who knew how many others were killed in the blast. This war was turning into something he didn't want to deal with anymore.

Michael and Rey sat on the couch in silence for the longest time just watching the news in horror.

Skyler came down the stairs a while later. "Kax is resting, she's had a stressful day. She will tell you about it later." He sat down on the couch. "So how are you two doing?"

"We are still on edge. Rey is going to sleep in the basement tonight. She is staying until we know it is safe."

Skyler was about to reply to Michael when his communicator went off. He walked to the other side of the couch and grabbed it. Right before he answered it, he said. "Sounds good, you make yourself at home, I got to take this." He answered his communicator, "Hello, Captain Therris speaking."

"Skyler? Don't answer the phone like that it bugs me and it's not proper, but I will let it slide this time. It's Cane, by the way, I'm happy that you didn't get hurt. Is everyone else fine? I saw your car driving around during the attack."

Skyler could hear the panting and the worry in his voice. "Sorry sir it's a habit and all of us are fine. Michael was the one driving my car he got out of there just in time. I heard about Thompson on the news."

Cane's voice dropped. "It was a horrible way for such a great man to die. They mutilated his body in such a humiliating fashion."

Skyler sighed. "It is a very tragic event and the world is not going to be the same without him. This war is getting out of hand."

"That's called war." Cane let out a deep sigh. "Skyler, I don't want you to hate me, but winter holidays are coming up in the next month and I want you to go home and see your mother. I think it's time you go back before it is too late."

Shaking his head, it sickened him to think about his mother and childhood home. "Well I haven't thought about plans for holidays yet, sir, but then I could see about it."

"I really want you to go see your mother, you never know." Cane said.

"Thank you, Cane, for your concern." He then turned off the communicator.

Michael and Rey had gone into the kitchen to get themselves something to eat.

Skyler walked into the kitchen and helped himself to a beer from the fridge and sat down at the table with the others.

Michael looked at Skyler. "I guess that was Cane checking to see if we are okay?"

Skyler took a gulp on his beer. "Ya, he saw you and thought it was me. He's in shock right now. I think a lot of us are." He took another gulp and finished the beer and got up to get another one. Skyler was holding a new beer in his hand when his communicator went off, again. He looked at the ID on it. It was his mother. He chugged half the beer down before he answered. "Hello, this is Skyler."

An angry male voice was on the other end. "You're still alive, I see. You made me look like a fool at the funeral not showing up you know that, right?"

Finishing the beer, he kindly replied. "Oh, it's you Charles, nice to hear from you. I'm glad you are so concerned about my well-being." Skyler walked out of the room to continue this conversation.

"Listen you little punk, I'm only calling because your mother asked me to. I don't care if you're dead or alive." His stepfather snapped into the phone.

Rolling his eyes back and holding the device away from his head. "Well if I was dead, I hope you never come to my funeral. I saw you on the news a few weeks ago, you have aged."

Charles barked into the phone. "You were always a thorn in my side. I hope the next attack you do die in."

Skyler scoffed. "You want the Cass to knock me off? Why don't you just come over here and finish the job yourself, since you never wanted me as a son."

Charles was silent. "You're not my son."

Skyler smirked. "I'm glad I'm not." He hung up the phone and walked back into the kitchen going for another beer.

Michael had a puzzled look on his face. "I know you probably do not want to talk about it but who was that?"

Skyler gulped down half a beer then looked at Michael. "Charles my wonderful stepdad wishing me dead."

Michael's jaw dropped. "Did he really?"

Nodding his head and finishing his beer. "Ya, he only called because my mother made him. He was hoping my body was mutilated like Fleet Admiral Thompson. Isn't he great, nothing ever changes with him."

Michael got up and blocked the fridge. "I think your drinking that beer a little fast. I think it is time, we all got some sleep, okay?"

Skyler tried to move Michael away from the fridge, then gave up. "Maybe you are right, see you two in the morning that's when we will know more details."

Chapter 22

Less than a week after the assassination of Fleet Admiral Thompson was the funeral. The gang once again had to wear their dress uniforms.

Skyler finally ha his own belt to wear, the only thing that was off was his medals had not been mounted yet. Trying to get them all pinned on in order.

Michael came into the room and watched Skyler struggle to put on his medals. "It is not that hard you know, that right?"

Skyler turned and glared at Michael. "Oh, really then how about you do it."

Michael walked over to Skyler and pinned all five medals on Skyler's uniform. "Why have not you gotten them mounted yet?"

Skyler frowned. "Same reason you haven't it takes two weeks and we have been busy. Once things calm down I will."

Michael laughed. "I know, but you have more than me. So, I thought I would bug you."

Kax walked into the room. "Come on guys it's time to get going. You know we must be there early because of seating. Officers on one side Cadets on the other. Politicians on one spot Civilians and press in another."

Skyler's eyes widened. "What do you mean Politicians?"

Kax sighed. "Politicians and Royal Family sorry this is a big deal it's not just anyone who died he is the Fleet Admiral he held this job for almost Fifty years. The King is even going to be there."

Shit, Charles will be there. Skyler's heart stopped. "I know this is a funeral, but I think we should bring our guns, at least, keep them in the car, too many important people are there. All it takes is one bomb and boom, everyone's dead."

A look of worry fell over Michael's face. "Normally I would be against this, but I agree with Skyler. Security will be tightened, and our entire families will be there."

Kax looked down. "I didn't think of it that way."

Skyler covered his face and groaned. "Great my mother and step-dad in the same room as me. That's been a long time. But on the plus side, the princess will be there."

Michael shook his head. "I thought you did not want to be with a princess? Also, I think it is just the King and Queen I do not think the rest will be there, maybe the crown prince."

Skyler combed his hair in the mirror. "A duchess no, but the actual princess. Well she would be worth giving it a try with."

Kax rolled her eyes. "The princess isn't interested in a one-night stand. The prince maybe, I heard he gets around."

Skyler snorted. "You're pregnant. You don't stand a chance with the prince."

"Could be. We're not sure yet." Kax pointed out.

Michael straightened his uniform. "You two are terrible. We are going to a funeral and you are more worried about who's getting laid. And how did Kax get pregnant I am still confused on that part?"

Skyler narrowed his eyes at Kax "You didn't tell him?"

Kax sighed. "I'm still hoping there's a mistake. I had sex with a random guy, got knocked up and were telling people Skyler is the father."

Michael raised an eyebrow at the pair. "You are really agreeing to this arrangement? What are you two going to tell your families?"

Skyler and Kax shared a look.

"I don't plan on telling my mother about any of this. She's out of my life." Skyler said.

Kax's hands shook with worry. "If it is real, I will have to tell my dad but not until I see the specialist."

Kax followed Michael. "You are right, this is serious, but we better get going, come on Skyler."

Skyler's hands shook. *Shit, David's going to hate me. Making him think I knocked up his daughter, he might kill me.* "Ya, waiting for a second opinion is best."

"Well I wish you two the best of luck. I will help in any way I can." Michael replied. "Now come on were going to be late."

The grounds were full. There was almost no place to park. They got there on time for setting up. It was six in the morning and the crowds were coming. The gang went to the officers' parade square to find out where they needed to be.

Kax went up to one of the men in a gray uniform who were holding tablets on the parade square. "Hello sir, me and my friends were wondering where we are supposed to line up?"

The man looked Kax over. "What fleet are you in?"

She replied. "Cane's fleet, sir."

The man looked at the chart. "Cane's fleet is not part of this parade. You want to go all the way to the other side of the square. From there you will be designated by your division."

"Thank you, sir." They all headed to the other side.

All the officers and Cadets who were on Earth and who could make it there on the square. They were all in their dress and divided into divisions. It was one rainbow of crowds. The sun was barely up, but this had to be done. Leading the parade was Thompson's fleet. And then it was Davis' and Cane's side by side. They had the officers lined up by rank and division first and in the front followed by cadets in order by name and division.

Michael parted from the gang once he saw the Engineering Cadets.

Kax and Skyler walked trying to find their place in the Command section. They saw another gray officer with a tablet and went up to him.

"Therris, and Tillion here, sir." Skyler said tall and proud.

The officer looked at his chart. "Therris you are in back next to Therrance. Tillion you are not in their area you are with the pilots you have to go to the group near the hangar."

Skyler waved to Kax as she walked away. He got into the line formation. There were in rows of ten and they continued till they were stopped. Skyler looked around at all the groups of people. There were not as many as he would have expected but who wanted to be on Earth anymore? Many had died in the attacks over the past few months and many more would die before this was over. So many officers were stationed on other planets and most of the older cadets were forced into early graduation. The forces needed everybody they could get to fight this war. The square was full, and the parade was about to start. All of them were at attention and waiting for the bagpipes to blow its pipes and they would be on their way. The officer in command would lead out first followed by the cadets. Then followed by the Science officers and their cadets. Then it was medical, security, ground and last of all engineering.

The Officers never made it into the hall. The building was so full of Politicians, their families and important figures. This was the first death of a Fleet Admiral in almost fifteen years. The higher officials knew who the next fleet admiral was, but the rest of the forces had not been notified who would take Thompson's place.

Fleet Admiral Thompson's body was not in the hall it had already been sent to be with his family and buried in a prerequisite area. But there was a huge poster-sized picture of him on the wall. And the bodies of the other fallen officers and cadets were placed in the caskets. All in matching brown oak coffins. With a small eight by ten photo in a silver frame of the fallen person. The death toll was in the thousands, from the beginning of this school year. It was worse than before. So many young people with their lives ahead of them were dying and there was nothing no one could do about it.

The world's elite gave their speeches. The King, the President, the Fleet Admirals, and many more made speeches. There were two giant view screens set up on the outside of the building, so the people outside could see. Every television station in federation was broadcasting this funeral. At the end of the service all the pilots flew in the sky for one last tribute to the fallen people.

The parade and services were over. There was a dinner going on afterward in the cafeteria and main hall for people. Skyler was starving, but he was more worried about finding his friends and staying out of sight from his mother. Wandering through the crowd, he headed to the hangar to find out where Kax was.

Pushing his way to the crowd he stopped when he saw a familiar face. He tried to hide as he saw his mother straight ahead of him. She looked right at him. He turned away hoping she didn't see him, but she did.

"Hello, Skyler you look nice in your uniform." She said bitterly.

He turned and looked right at her. "It's nice to see you too, mother. I'm glad you were concerned with my safety with this last attack."

She turned her head. "I always worry that's why I don't want you here. You know I lived through the last two wars and served in one. I know what they're like."

He glared at her. "You really think I'm going to quit after three years and five medals? I'm good at what I do, this is my life. If I die doing it, then I will die happy!"

She shook her head. "You sound like your father when you talk like that. That is the stupid attitude that got him killed."

Shocked and angry at his mother. "Are we really going to talk about this here, in public, at a funeral?" That was the first time he had heard her mention his father like that. "Speaking of my Father you didn't tell me he had an urn and that he had been so close to me all this time." He could see the hurt expression on her face.

The Earth stopped when she heard his words. "I didn't know, I mean I didn't want to tell you, I…"

He shot her a dangerous glare. If his eyes could reflect on how he was feeling inside they would be burning with flames. "Just when I try to think maybe you do care and its just Charles who hates me you do something like this."

With tearful eyes, she reached out to give her son a hug in apology.

He stepped back.

Kax came running up to Skyler and gave him a hug.

Skyler hugged Kax back. He was glad she was there at the right time he didn't want his mother to touch him.

Kax let go as soon as she saw Skyler's mother. She lightly smiled holding out her hand. "So, we meet again, Mrs. Therris"

His mother snarled at Kax's hand refusing to shake it. "It's Mrs. Roux now, you little tramp."

Skyler's body filled with rage. He clenched his fists.

Offended Kax snapped back before Skyler had a chance to respond. "I'm not a tramp, how dare you say that when you don't even know anything about me!"

Sandy stood firm. "I know exactly who you are. You're Kax Tillion daughter of Karmantha and David Tillion. Your mother, my husband's pilot, was his whore till her death. All the women my son hangs out with are whores, so you must take after your mother."

Kax's face turned red with rage she reached out her hand to scratch Sandy's face. Skyler held her back. "How dare you say that about my mother you bitch!"

Skyler held Kax back as best as he could. He didn't know why. He wanted to rip his mom's head off too. "Kax is not a whore she is the most decent girl I have ever met. Now leave before, I let her go."

"She looks like a whore with that belly, I hope she's just fat. By the way Skyler, I expect you home for the holidays this year come alone," His mother snorted and turned away.

Once she was out of site, Skyler hugged Kax. Holding her tight. "I'm so sorry she said those things to you."

"My mother wasn't a whore." Crying in his arms she looked up at Skyler with her eyes red, puffy and full of tears. "I'm not showing, am I? She was just being mean, right?"

"I know that, your mother was a good person." Skyler brushed the hair away from her face and kissed her on the forehead. He looked down at her belly, which before today he hadn't paid attention too. "There is a little bump forming. I think the doctor might have been right or it could be gas. But you will be fine you got me."

She looked up into Skyler's eyes and began to cry. Skyler held her close.

Michael came over he had finally found them. "Hey there, did I miss something?"

Kax broke off from her and Skyler's embrace. Wiping the tears off her face. "Skyler's mom is a bitch."

Skyler coughed. "That's an understatement."

"I was wondering are we staying to eat or going home?" Michael asked.

Skyler's stomach rumbled. "There are too many people here. I think we are all hungry let's go to the city and get something to eat. How does that sound?"

Michael smiled. "Okay but can we go to that new whole food restaurant I still want to try it out?"

Skyler smirked. "As long as I can order a steak, I don't think a salad will fill me up."

Chapter 23

The next day at school Kax went right to Fleet Admiral Cane's office to talk to him about her potential pregnancy. She didn't have to talk to him, normally she could have just gone to the Admiral of the Piloting department. But she knew what they would say. They would tell her she would have to cut back on her piloting studies and withdraw her application for deep space training. She wasn't going to let a baby stop her from achieving her dreams. She knew if anyone would understand her and help her Cane would be the one to talk to. She waited in the waiting room until Cane was ready to see her.

He opened his office door and called out. "Cadet Tillion you may come in now."

Kax entered the office. She was silent holding her belly. She took a seat.

Cane sat down at his desk. "So Kax what seems to be the issue?"

Kax placed her hand on her stomach. "I might be pregnant."

Cane raised an eyebrow. "Congratulations but why are you coming to me about this? Shouldn't you talk to Admiral Miller?"

She sighed. "I thought about it, but I wanted to come to you first. I'm waiting to see a Catillion specialist to confirm and to tell me what I should do because the baby is mixed. Then I will know for sure. But I still want to be a pilot and do my deep space training."

Cane pinched the bridge of his nose. "You know why the rules state that a pregnant woman can't train to be a pilot, especially a deep space pilot right? Because being a pilot is dangerous lots of things could go wrong for a regular cadet. The forces will not risk the life of an unborn child. You will have to turn it down."

"I know that sir and that's why I came to you. Catillion pregnancies don't last long only about 6months so if they prove I am pregnant I will be recovered in time for this summer to do this training." She pleaded, "All I ever wanted to do was become a deep space pilot and you know I'll do well at it."

Cane let out a deep sigh. "You are right but deep space piloting in very risky what are we to do with the baby if something happens to you? Also, it is very long hours you won't be around enough to take care of the baby. You will spend sometimes days away from the base. Last I checked you weren't married; do you know who the father is?"

She put her head down. She couldn't tell him it was Jake, but she wasn't sure she should lie. She looked up at Cane. "It's Skyler, he's the father."

Cane stared at her in shock for a few moments. "I see, he's got an interesting future ahead of himself too." He thought for a long moment. "I'll leave your file as it is right now. But as soon as you find out if your pregnant or not you come to me. If you are I will have to pull you from the program. If not, I would recommend talking to the doctor about getting some sort of birth control. I can't force you to take it, but I can advise if you don't want to be in this position again protect yourself."

She nodded her head. "Yes sir."

***

Skyler was sitting alone in the cafeteria. *Damnit where is everyone? I never eat lunch alone.* He picked at his meatloaf slowly.

His heart stopped, and chills went down his spine when he felt a hand with long claw-like nails touch his back.

"Long time no see," Nancy said. She took a seat next to Skyler. She placed her hand on his leg. "Mind if I join you?" She took a piece of meatloaf off his plate and popped it into her mouth.

Skyler quickly jerked away from her. "What are you doing here Nancy. Leave me alone or I will report you!"

She laughed reaching for his blond hair. "Report me for what? If you report me, you will also get in trouble for being in my room after hours. I don't think you want that."

Skyler kept himself more than an arms-distance away from her. "What do you want from me, Nancy?"

She gave a devilish grin. "Rey, I hear she is dating Michael now. I figure that was your idea. I want her back and you're going to get her back for me."

Skyler shook his head. "Fat chance. Rey is her own person and she can date whoever she wants. Also, after the way you treated her and me, I don't think she is going to go back to you ever."

Nancy took the fork off Skyler's plate and danced it along the meatloaf. "You have been hanging around Kax a lot more. I wonder what that's about? Has she finally given into you? It would be a shame if someone took her away from you." She stabbed the fork into the meatloaf.

No don't hurt Kax! I can't let Kax be in danger, especially not with the baby. Skyler glared at her. "You leave Kax out of this. I don't control what Rey does, I'm not like you."

She glared. "Well if that's your choice." She got up and walked away.

Skyler's whole body shook in shock. "What do I do?" He whispered to himself. He got up from the table leaving his tray of unfinished food and walked off. "I got to make sure Kax is safe."

Chapter 24

Skyler walked past Michael's room. He saw through the open doorway Michael was getting dressed up. "Dude it is Friday night why are you getting dressed up?"

Michael shook his head. "I have another date with Rey she is really a nice girl you know that. My question to you it is Friday night, why are you not getting dressed up?"

"I promised to eat ice cream and watch movies with Kax all night." Skyler leaned on the doorway. "Wait isn't this is your third date, does that mean what I think it does?"

Michael shook his head. "No, we are just friends and are keeping it that way. I am taking her to a Cafe, and we are going to listen to amateur poetry. By the way I know the baby is not yours, but I am worried you are using this just as an excuse to get close to her? I mean I have never seen you act this way it is almost as if you think you could be the father?"

Should I warn him about Nancy? Skyler shook his head. "You're a boring date. And nah I'm still getting laid on the side. Not with Kax, maybe one day. She still doesn't think she is pregnant, but one more month and we find out for sure. It doesn't hurt to form a bond and be there for her. She needs someone to man up and help her through this difficult time."

Michael shrugged. "I guess you are right. I have never been around a pregnant woman before, so I have no idea. Just do not hurt her." Michael finished with his hair and headed out of the room.

Michael can handle Nancy. I'll protect Kax. Skyler moved out of the doorway. "I'm only concerned about her."

Michael walked down the stairs and headed towards the door. "Well I am off, see you later I will be back around midnight."

Kax walked into the living room with a bowl of popcorn and two pints of ice cream. She sat down the on the couch getting comfortable. "Come on Skyler the movie is going to start."

He waved goodbye to Michael and went over and hopped over the couch. "So what movie are we watching?" He grabbed a large hand full of popcorn and started shoving it in his mouth.

She turned the movie on with the remote. "It's a movie about this Modorlean girl who moves to Earth and is trying to make her way in a world full of smut."

Damn, I should have picked the movie. He groaned. "Please tell me this is a comedy at least?"

Waiting for their order. Michael looked across the table at Ray. "So how is the book I lent you?"

She looked at her glass of water. "Not to be mean but I'm not really interested in it. I'm so sorry."

Michael shook his head. "It is fine by me I do not mind."

Ray sighed. "Michael, I like you but well it's our third date and I want to know are you expecting something from me after dinner?"

His eyes popped, then frowned. "No! In no way, I thought that I was clear we are just friends and I said we were not going to do that."

She looked down at the empty space on the table. "Are you sure? Most people only want that. You're not into men, are you?"

"No!" Michael snapped, "I am tired of people assuming that I like men just because I do not want to sleep with them. I am asexual, I do not have sex. I see you as a friend I am a decent guy. Skyler told me about you, and he said for me to show you a good time without sex. You are a lovely girl and I like you a lot, but you are just a friend. Also, if I was going to sleep with you I would do it because I was truly in love with you. I barely know you, how can I love you?"

She looked up at Michael with sad eyes. "I have my own issues too. On why I want to sleep with you. But I guess it's fine for now."

Michael knew then it was time to get out of this relationship. He did the favor for Skyler and now it was time for him to move on. She clearly had been so abused that she couldn't understand when someone was just being nice to her. He thought she was a nice girl; she wasn't his type but still, he enjoyed her company.

***

Kax sat on the couch watching the movie. She reached into the popcorn bowl and returned empty handed. *Damn, why did Skyler have to eat all the popcorn so fast? I wish we had more.* She looked over and saw Skyler focused on the movie. *And he said he wasn't interested, ha.* She had been watching his actions the past few weeks since she found out she might be pregnant. He was being kinder to her. He was being very attentive and caring about her needs. But he was shying away from his goals in life he was focusing on her and not anything else. She knew that wasn't right. He might have agreed to raise the kid as his own, it was a flattering offer but not right for him. She couldn't say yes because he was trying to be something he wasn't. He was not old enough to be a father, she thought. *Making him a father now would distract him, he might never be a captain then. If I go for deep space training, I couldn't make him babysit and miss class because I'm training.* The decision was clear in her mind she couldn't let Skyler be the father. She had to find a way to get him back on focus.

But what about Michael? She thought. *Maybe I could ask him? The baby is half Squallite.* When they first met, she would have gone out with him but now she knew she wasn't her type. He was the kind of guy where you could trust him. He would always be there for you and stand up for you when you needed it. He was husband material but not 'her' husband material.

What am I thinking? Trying to get two men who aren't the father to raise my child. That's not right. You have one mother and one father or two parents not three. That's how my parents raised me. She let out a long sigh. *But I can't do this alone and I can't tell Jake.*

There is always my dad? She thought. *Would he be willing to raise my baby? How do I even tell him? My brother isn't well enough, and my sister wants nothing to do with kids.*

She didn't want to be a bad mother, but she wasn't seeing any other options. She wasn't a cadet who could take the baby with her if she wanted. But she was a cadet someone would have to stay home with the baby and watch it. She didn't feel right about having a nanny or babysitter watch her kid because she had to go to school. She didn't want to have a baby now. If it turned out she was pregnant, she would defiantly keep it but if she would have been smarter, she would have waited. This was all getting too much for her, she couldn't think with all her hormones running wild. She started to cry.

Skyler moved the popcorn bowl off her lap and leaned over and gave her a hug. "Hey, come on the movie isn't that sad she lost her job for what she believed in, that's a good thing."

She looked up at Skyler with her face covered in tears. "I'm not crying over the movie. I just don't know what to do with this baby if it is real? I can't be a new mother and go for deep space training. I would need a full-time babysitter."

Skyler looked down at her stomach and placed one had on her belly. "It will all be fine. I'll take care of the baby. That's what I'm here for. You don't have to do this alone."

Her sad eyes locked with Skyler's. "It's not your baby. I can't put the burden on you. I don't want to distract you from your career."

His smile faded and let out a sigh. He held her tight. "Well there is always your father, could he raise the baby?"

She looked back up at him with her nose all red and eyes puffy. "I could ask him, but it's still not fair to anyone. Why are you being so nice to me?"

He brushed the hair out of her face. "Because I was an unloved child. I don't know anything about babies or kids, but I know they need love. I also grew up without a father, my childhood was hard I don't want that for any child. Things will get better."

Kax began to cry. "You really are just a nice guy," she leaned over giving him a hug.

***

Michael came bursting through the door and stomped up the stairs to his room.

Skyler had never seen him this mad before. He called up to him. "How was the date?"

Michael shouted back. "Terrible! It is over and I am never seeing that girl again!"

Skyler was at a loss. He had a sad pregnant woman on the couch with him and an angry friend next to his bedroom. He didn't really know which way to go. Kax was still crying so slowly he got off the couch and quietly said. "You know what, I got to make a phone call." Like a rocket, he rushed into the kitchen and pulled out a can of beer from the fridge. As he took his first sip, he heard his communicator go off. He picked it up, without looking at the number, *Whoever is on the phone can't make things worse.* "Hello, this is Skyler."

A harsh voice was on the other line. "Hello Skyler, this is Charles how are you tonight?"

Hey, I was wrong, He finished his beer and laughed. "No, it couldn't be any worse."

Charles growled into the phone. "Anyway, I have been asked to invite you here for winter holidays."

Rolling his eyes. "You mean my mother is making you invite me. Because the last thing I remember you saying to me is '*Your little snot nose bastard, you ever come back to this house again I will shoot you for trespassing.*' So, you can see why I stayed away."

Charles groaned. "Well it is good to see you listened to me for once, Therris."

"Oh, so we're back to using my last name as an insult, are we?" Skyler snapped back. "You know I'm proud of my father and the legacy he left me. Even if you hate him. Maybe I would listen more if you treated me with respect and not like a piece of dirt. Oh, and speaking of last names when did you make my mother change her name to yours?"

Charles laughed. "When I became senator. It didn't look right for a senator to be married to a woman who had a different last name.

When you were living at home it was different, she kept her name for you, but she is Mrs. Roux now, my wife and you're just, Therris."

Skyler snarled. "You two were made for each other. I would've never taken your name, no matter what. I will be there for the holidays this year."

"That's fine you're not my son anyway." Charles scoffed. "Your mother will be pleased." He hung up the phone.

Skyler grabbed another beer out of the fridge. He was going to bed. There was no way he was going to stay up any longer and let this day get any worse.

Chapter 25

"Judson? What do you mean Judson is Thompson's replacement? That's not fair he was supposed to replace me, your highness!" Cane shouted furiously.

The King looked at Cane. "Behave yourself, Cane. Judson is too old to wait for you to die and he is more than qualified to take Thompson position in the forces. I know this is a bit of a shock to you, but there is nothing you can do about it."

Cane sat back down in his seat in front of the King's desk. "It is just out of the highest ranks, Judson is the only one I trust to replace me, your majesty. There were so many other people who could take on the job and still would have been good."

The King shook his head. "But not with the knowledge he has. You have the experience. Davis has the strength and Judson has the knowledge. You three will make a great team."

Cane slouched in his seat. "Does Fleet Admiral Davis know about the change yet?"

The King nodded. "Yes, she was notified this morning. Through video chat. Since she is still on Virgo Three helping out with the new cadets at the new base."

Cane nodded. "I know, where will Judson be stationed?"

Looking at some papers on his desk. "Earth for now, and this will be made public in January after exams. At the start of the new semester, is that understood?"

Cane agreed. "Yes, your highness."

Chapter 26

Kax shook Skyler awake. "Come on Skyler is almost noon you said you would be up by now."

Skyler moaned and groaned getting up out of the bed. "Kax why are you rushing me? You know I have a hangover."

Kax rolled her eyes. "You promised me I could get your room ready for my dad when you woke up. It is noon he will be here at two I don't have time to wait no more. Don't you have to be somewhere too?"

Skyler brushed his hair back and got out of his bed. It was the day he dreaded 'Winter holidays' were here, and he had to go to his mother's. "Why don't you give him Michael's room and I just stay here. And sleep till new years."

Kax shoved his clothes at him. "You take your clothes and get out. You know I can't take Michael's room he is staying for a few more days he has some work to finish. Then he is leaving you said, you would leave as soon as you could. So, get out!"

Skyler rolled his eyes. "Guess you really are pregnant with that attitude. You know we have a guest room."

"The guest room is too cold in the winter." The rage burned in her eyes and she shoved Skyler into the hallway. "GET OUT NOW!" She slammed the door behind him.

Standing in the hallway in his lime green boxers he started to put his black t-shirt and blue jeans on. He went downstairs to the kitchen. He saw Michael sitting there playing with his tablet. "Dude, could you break my leg or something for me?"

Michael looked up at Skyler. "Why would I do an idiotic thing like that?"

Skyler shrugged grabbed a slice of leftover pizza out of the fridge. It was cold, but he liked it that way. "I don't know, maybe because I don't want to go to my mother's place."

Michael shook his head at Skyler. "No, just no. You had the chance to turn them down you chose to go, so man up. It really sucks to leave but you dug your own grave."

Skyler sat down at the table with Michael rubbing his head. "I wouldn't be going, but Cane said I should. I don't know why I mean she barely talked to me in the last five years and this year she is insisting what is going on?"

Michael examined at Skyler. "How old is your mother?"

Skyler counted on his greasy pizza figures. "Fifty I think, why does it matter?"

Michael shook his head. "I thought maybe she was pregnant or something. But I think she is too old. Now do not hate me, I only thought that because when looking up Senator Charles Roux online, he has no children, never has. He is a senator. All current senators have kids it shows they are family men. And well he never adopted you or listed you anywhere I found. Also, he got your mother to change her name-"

"Shut up!" Skyler took the tablet from Michaels' hands. He read over the article on the screen. "You're right it mentions my mother but not that she has a kid. I'm really left out." He searched up his father, all he got was only a few news articles and service records. He went back to the news articles. He found one that had a picture of him and his mother at the funeral. He passed it back to Michael. "There you go, I found me."

Michael cringed at the pizza grease on his screen. He looked at the article. "How weird that this is it."

Skyler shrugged. "Who knows. But my mother isn't having kids she had a chance to when they got married and she turned him down. She told me she didn't want any more kids. I was too much to handle, without my father."

Michael stared at Skyler. "So, you were always the little hellraiser. If it is not a baby what is it?"

***

Michael's words haunted Skyler as he drove up to Mother's house. He loved this house, it had so many memories of his father and childhood. He loved the white picket fence that went around the entire yard. He drove past the white milk-carton 2.5 story farmhouse with its two large bay windows in the front. He pulled the car to the side of the house. Front of the attached double garage.

It pained him to see how much the vibe of the place had changed since Charles came around when he was twelve. He parked his car in front of the garages and walked in. The kitchen had been repainted, but the layout was the same. The walls used to be a pale yellow were now a dusted rose. He looked at the hardwood counters in an L along the wall with matching cupboards. He walked past the small room to the light blue dining room. He didn't hear any sounds in the house. Turned at the hall went straight up the stairs by passing his old room right up to the attic. It didn't look like anything had been touched since he was last there when he was fifteen the dust and cobwebs blanketed the boxes.

His little cot was still there. The cot he had watched the stars from for so many nights. It was his cot. The cot that was placed right under the bay window. He had lost his virginity here. He walked up to it and dusted the top blanket off and sat down. He looked up at the gray winter sky.

He wished it would snow. He loved snow it was cold and wet, but peaceful. Snow knew how to fall with grace. Its cold kisses knew how to remind you that you were alive. Only about five winters he could remember there being snow during the holidays. He wished that there was more.

As he lay on the on the cot he started to drift off. He knew he had a bedroom, but this was always his real room. He heard the front door slam shut. He quickly jumped off the cot and ran out of the attic. His mother knew he went up there, but Charles.

He met Charles at the bottom of the old creaky wooden stairs. Skyler stared into Charles dark cold eyes circled with crow's feet. He didn't say anything to the politician in a black suit.

Charles stared Skyler down. "You have grown up well I see. You still look like your father. Which is a shame, it makes you look dumber than you are."

He scoffed at Charles. "Aw man, you had to say something like that, just when I thought you might actually be nice over the holidays. Well, here's all I have to say to you. You're an asshole."

Charles just looked at Skyler. "Your mother is not going to be here for the next three days. She was called back into work. I, on the other hand, will be here. Just thought I would let you know."

Letting out a long sigh. "Well the house is big enough I don't think we will even notice each other."

Charles shook his head. "I converted your room into an office, you will have to sleep on the couch, so avoiding each other will be harder than you think."

He looked behind him at the small living room with the old brown couch. Trying to be on his best behavior. "That's no problem with me. If you don't mind now I think, I'm going to go for a walk." Skyler quickly walked past Charles and headed out the door. Once outside he took a deep breath. The temperature dropped so he went into his car and pulled out his cadet jacket, the country was much colder than the city. He walked down the road. The old path to the downtown area of the one-hover car community. The trees might have grown, but nothing had changed it was still the same. It felt weird coming back this one spot of the world still seemed like it was stuck in the 2160's when the rest of the world changed. Sure, the homes were equipped with solar panels and other modern technologies but everything else seemed to be so old and out of date when it was only less than an hour out of the city.

Strolling down main street he strolled past the old-style homes that were built long before anyone alive could remember, all historic homes now. Like his mother's house, it was historic. His father had bought that house for his mother after they got married. His dad wanted a modern penthouse in the city, but his mother wanted a quiet country home. *She always got her way.* Skyler saw the old

148

convenience store. It brought back memories of when he used to go in there and try and convince the shop owner that he was old enough to drink when the guy had known Skyler all his life. He continued to walk down memory lane. Looking at all the farmhouses all different colors.

He walked further down the street. He saw the old to one level school he uses to go to from kindergarten to the middle school. His high school was out of town right on the edge of the city. This was just a small place with around 600 kids. His high school had over 5000. He walked through the yard. Remembering the good old days before everything in his life went tragically wrong.

The school bell rang, and the kids all began to leave. He hadn't been in school for so long that he had forgotten the kids would be getting out of school at this time for their holidays. He tried to stay out of the way by leaving the grounds. But just then he saw a light brown-haired green-eyed girl he used to know. She was standing at the doorway watching the kids leave the school. *She must be a teacher now.* He thought. He walked back up to the school. As he got closer, he caught her eye. He smiled and walked right up to her. "Hey Mandy, long time no see, your looking fine."

"Is that you Skyler?" She laughed when she saw Skyler's winning smile. "You haven't changed, have you?"

Skyler shrugged. "Well depends on how you mean that. I'm a lot older, I have more experience and-"

"And you still have high expectations, don't you? Oh, Skyler, you're a sight for sore eyes. I see you have joined the galactic forces, just like you always said you would." She said smiling back.

He showed off his jacket. "Yup I'm a third-year cadet right now. And you're a teacher how did you get to be a teacher so young?"

"Hard work and I'm a year older than you remember. So, I worked hard getting my grades and doing extra courses, this is my first year as a teacher so it's not like I have been doing this for years."

"Really? So, do you think you can teach me a few things?" He winked.

She playfully shoved Skyler away from her. "I didn't say yes to you in school I'm not going to say yes to you now."

He laughed back. "I remember but you were a virgin back then. I'm glad you found something you love doing."

"I do love it. The kids are fun, and it just gives me so much joy to help teach these kids. So, I guess you're back home for the holidays?"

He looked down at his feet. "I guess you could say that."

"Still having problems with Charles? That's sad. Actually, I'm surprised he is still around."

"Well, he hasn't changed. But I'm here not much else to do. Everyone at the academy has left. People either went to be with their families or used their transporter credits to go on vacation."

She nodded and looked back and winked at him as she went back into the school. "Why don't you come in and we will talk about this. The kids are gone, but we can still hang out in the school after hours."

Skyler followed her into the school. "You know the last girl who said that to me I ended up, well I think you can guess."

Chapter 27

Tired and frustrated Skyler rolled around on the couch trying to get some sleep. It was just too hard the couch didn't feel right. He laid there. He did want to be here. He loved the house but not who lived there. The couch was hard and lumpy, almost like Charles did something to the couch.

He got up off the couch. He wasn't going to sleep here no matter what anyone said. Quietly, he went up the stairs and into the attic. Not caring about the spiders and other bugs that might be up there just that he knew the cot was more comfortable than a couch that felt like it was packed with rocks.

Laying down on the cot he looked out of the window at the night sky. Watching the stars twinkle has was always been his favorite thing. Finally having a place to lay down that was comfortable, he fell asleep in no time. Peacefully he slept the rest of the night.

Skyler awoke to an angry face glaring down on him. Not sure what to do so he smiled at Charles. "Good morning, did you sleep well?"

Charles glared. "You were to sleep on the couch, not in the attic. This attic has been locked off it's not yours."

Rolling his eyes, not moving on the cot. "I would have slept on the couch, but you stuffed it with rocks. I knew there was an old cot in the attic, so I came here. What is the problem? I didn't bother you when you were asleep so who cares where I sleep?"

Charles yanked the blanket off Skyler. "Get up and don't come up here again."

Cold now that he didn't have a blanket Skyler jumped off the cot and stared into Charles cold dark eyes. "You're and such an asshole."

Charles looked at his almost naked stepson. He pushed him over the cot. "Don't speak to me like that your ungrateful brat."

Skyler hit his head on the wall behind him. He struggled to get up. His leg now had a small cut on the back from getting scratched by a loose nail. Once he got up he noticed the pain in his spine. He saw Charles walking away. Skyler ran over and jumped Charles knocking him on the ground.

Charles tried to push Skyler off him. "You little brat!" He rolled them over. He pinned Skyler down, sitting on his legs. He punched Skyler in the face.

Skyler winced at the pain and fear filled his eyes.

Charles stood up a moment later. He kicked Skyler in the ribs. "You have twenty minutes to get out of this house and off this property or I'm getting my gun."

Skyler didn't take his eyes off Charles as he left the attic. Once Charles was gone. Skyler groaned in pain. His back ached, and his leg was bleeding. He got up and slowly got dressed. His body hurt all over. Putting on his clothes, he looked out at the view in the window one last time. He knew this was going to be his last time here, at least for a very long time.

Getting into his car he drove off without a goodbye. Not sure where he was going but anywhere but here was good for him. *I can't go to Michaels not even sure where he lives. Kax has her dad over and I don't want to bother them. I told her already I would be nice and stay away. Perry is working on his plants. I don't want to call Leon. He told me to come here. If he knows I left, he might get mad at me. I guess I only got one place left.*

He drove the car to his uncle's mansion. The front gate let him in. Once he was in there, he saw his uncle in a rush with a suitcase. "Hey, Uncle Justin is it okay I stay for the holidays?"

Justin smiled putting his suitcase down. "I'm going to guess things didn't work out with Charles. Yes, you can stay here but I won't be here I have a few functions to go to but enjoy yourself." He gave his nephew a hug. "I really must be going, okay I'm running late for my flight, enjoy your stay. It's good to see you again."

Skyler waved goodbye to his uncle and sighed. *Alone again.* This holiday season was really beginning to suck. *Why did Cane tell me to go to my mother's house in the first place?* He had avoided going home all these years he knew that it would just end in disaster. But there was nothing he could do about it now.

Chapter 28

Skyler spent the next couple of days alone in the mansion. This place had everything he needed, except someone to cuddle. There were a few maids around the house to keep it clean in case a speck of dust was found. None of the maids seemed to catch his attention, it would have been nice if at least one was hot and easy.

Laying on the couch in the billiard room drinking some scotch. He lay there relaxing and just trying to enjoy the silence. About to fall asleep from boredom when his phone went off. He picked up the communicator and answered it. "Hello, this is Skyler."

"Skyler this is your mother why are you not at the house for the holidays you said you would be?" Her irritable voice rang in Skyler's ears.

"I was there, ask Charles. He kicked me out. He also threatened to shoot me if I came back."

Letting out an annoyed sigh. "There you go again making up stories, you can come home I want to see you, son."

Rubbing his temples. "No, I'm not making up stories and I will not go back there. Sorry but you have to live without me, mother."

She groaned into the phone. "Sometimes you are so difficult, Skyler. Is it so hard to ask you for one family holiday together?"

He nodded even though she couldn't see him. "Ya it is, mother, and that's all there is to it. Sorry, but I will not be coming back no matter what you say."

A sadness filled her voice. "Are you at your Uncle's? Can I come visit? There is something very important I need to talk to you about."

He let out a deep sigh. "Yes, I am, and you can come talk to me. But don't bring Charles."

"I will leave him at home. I just need to talk to you about something important, I will see you in a bit."

Hanging up the phone he finished the last quarter of scotch in the bottle and got ready to see his mother.

***

He met his mother in the main hall, she saw him and gave him a hug. Not hugging her back. He shifted out of her arms. "Okay mother, you said you wanted to talk to me what is it?"

Letting go she frowned at her son. "Please, Skyler, don't be like that, this is important let's go and sit down."

They walked to the dining hall and sat down at the large twelve-seater hardwood table. They sat across from each other at one of the ends.

Skyler looked at her. He felt as if he was being dragged here against his will. "So, what is so important?"

Shaking her head, she let out a sigh. "You know how I told you that I didn't want more kids because you were too much to handle?"

His heart raced and sweat ran down his for heard. He was afraid of what she might say next. "More like you wouldn't let me forget."

She looked down at her hands. "Skyler, Charles is getting older and he has never had a son. He wants to run for president one day and it looks good if he is a family man. Since you have never wanted to be his son well…"

Skyler's heart stopped, and his eyes bulged. "What did you do?"

She put one hand on her stomach and held out the other to hold Skyler's hand. "Skyler I'm pregnant. With your brother."

A sharp pain went through his chest, he started to breathe heavy. His head went dizzy. *How can she have a baby with that asshole?*

She put her hand on his arm, "Skyler this is a good thing. We can be a family"

Skyler jerked away from his mother's touch. "Don't touch me. Mother I don't think this is a good idea." Rubbing his head in shock he mumbled, "I need a drink"

His mother's eyes widen. "Since when do you drink?"

Skyler turned and looked at his mother. "I have been drinking since I was fourteen, it's normal for me. I guess you never noticed how many times I came home drunk or had a hangover the next day. But that is not the point you are having Charles baby why? Your too old and you're working, he's working you barely raised me. How are you going to raise the baby?"

Giving him a nasty glare, she took a deep breath to calm a little down. "I could either take an extended maturity leave or retire early. As a commodore, I will get a pretty decent pension. I was there for you when you were growing up don't you remember?"

Skyler buried his head in his face. "No, you weren't there for me. When you were working, I had Charles and when both were busy you dropped me off at Uncle Justin's. Mom, you didn't even know I drank and had sex as a teenager."

Her jaw dropped, and she snapped back. "And what, now I'm supposed to know you're sleeping with that cat whore?"

Skyler scoffed and rolled his eyes. "No mother she's a friend. I have been having sex since I was fourteen and have been with countless women."

She put her hand over her face and started to cry. "How did I miss all this?"

Skyler shrugged. "Well, for one thing, mother you never listen to me. Second, you are always working. Do you even know why I moved out?"

His mother took a deep breath. "Charles told me you were a moody teenager who wanted his own space."

He burst out laughing not sure if he should find that funny or disturbing. "No, Charles beat me. He always hit me. He hates me because he hates my father. He doesn't want me, and he beat me one too many times and told me to get out or he would shoot me. He did it again a few days ago because he found me sleeping in the attic." He pointed to the bruise on his cheek. "See this he gave this to me."

She took a deep breath and shook her head. "Charles is not like that he wanted you as his son you always fought with him. He is a good man. I know he slapped you a few times, but you were out of hand. You were always a wild kid. But it doesn't matter now. You made your choice. You choose to move on without me or your family. I hope you enjoy the frontlines because that's where they send freshly graduated cadets." She got up and stomping out of the room.

"Thanks for caring." He called out to her as she disappeared out of sight.

Alone and in the room, he felt like getting out of his seat and grabbing a beer, but his legs wouldn't move. He was paralyzed. He started to cry. Not wanting to call anyone but he wanted to be with someone. Someone just for the moment to hold him and make him feel whole again that he was real and there was someone who cared. He tilted his head back staring up at the light brown ceiling. He was so alone.

Chapter 29

"Thanks, you have no idea what this means to me," Skyler said.

Michael sighed. "You are my friend. I am doing what any good friend would do."

"You do know I'm not trying to interrupt your time with your father." Skyler slouched in the passenger seat of his car.

"I know. I had a feeling you would be calling when you went to your mom's." Michael drove a little faster. It was a long trip from Skyler's uncles to his place. "Will my bike be safe at your uncle's?"

"Ya, he has great security." Skyler sighed. "You were right. My mother is pregnant."

Michael took his eyes off the road. "Seriously? I am so sorry."

Skyler rubbed his temples. "Ya, and for the exact same reason you stated. Now I have to deal with a pregnant mother and Kax."

"What is the problem? I mean you are not raising your mom's kid so what is the problem with her and Kax both being pregnant?"

"It's the fact that Kax's baby is the same age as Charles' spawn. I don't want to become a father the same year Charles does." Skyler shuddered with disgust. "Are we almost there?"

"You know I live on almost the other side of the megacity, right? You live on the east end I'm on the west."

"Central. I'm central I'm closer to Rochester and you are near London neighborhood." Skyler pointed out.

"Compared to me you are east but yes the city goes a lot farther east." Michael turned the car into a neighborhood that was old run down and unkept. There were broken streetlamps and potholes on the road.

"I'm glad this is a hover car. Is this where you live?" Skyler asked.

"I wish, my neighborhood is worse. Don't worry your car will be safe. They will know you are my guest." Michael responded.

"I thought London neighborhood was a good area?"

"I am not in London I am outside London. My neighborhood was a nice trailer park campsite. But the city expanded built the homes we just saw, but they expanded too fast, so they were sold for cheap. The wealth of the area made mine drop and now no one wants to live out here." Michael pulled the car up to the trailer. "Were here."

Skyler grabbed his bag out of the back of the car. "That's it?"

Michael shot Skyler a glare. "Sorry it is not a mansion like your uncle's. But it has two rooms and the kitchen table turns into a bed for guests."

"That's not what I meant. I just thought it was a small house, not a trailer. Size of the house doesn't bother me. I'm sorry if I offended you." Skyler said.

"When you live in one of the worst areas in the city you get teased a lot about where you live. It might not be the best, but it is better than nothing." Michael walked up the ramp into the trailer. "Hey, we are here."

Sam was sitting at the kitchen table with his wheelchair next to his seat. "Hey son, and Skyler. It's nice to see you again."

Skyler went over the table and sat down across from Sam. He shook his hand. "It is nice to see you too. Thank you for letting me stay here for the holidays."

"Christmas has always been a time to take in people in need," Sam said.

Michael went over to the counter and put on a kettle of water. "Skyler, would you like some tea?"

"Do you have any beer?" Skyler asked.

Michael frowned. "No, we do not keep alcohol in the house."

Sam cleared his throat. "Michael go to my nightstand and go into the third drawer only there is a bottle of rye we can share it."

"Dad when did you start drinking?" Michael went over and got the bottle.

"The bottle is mostly full. I only drink it on special occasions. And I think today is a good day."

Michael got them two glasses and set the bottle on the table.

Skyler and Sam clanked glasses. "So, Sam what is Christmas?"

Sam laughed. "Sorry I forgot it's a Christian holiday. It's the day we celebrate the birth of our lord and savior by putting up decorative trees and giving gifts to our loved ones. Happens once a year." He pointed to the twelve-inch Christmas tree on the kitchen counter.

Skyler stared at Sam in confusion. "Christian? That has to do with that thing Michael says he is, Catholic, right?"

Sam nodded. "Yes. Do you know what religion is?"

Skyler shook his head. "Never had one. Parents raised me without one. I know Michael has mentioned something about God? A few times but I have no idea what that means."

Sam nodded his head. "I'll lend you a book if you want to learn more. But let's just enjoy our time together and hang out."

Michael had finished making his tea and sat down at the table next to Skyler. The table went silent.

Skyler pulled a deck of cards out of his pocket. "Anyone want to play cards?"

Sam smiled. "Sounds like a good idea."

***

Late into the night, Skyler was laying in the table bed wide awake. At first, he thought it was the bed but soon realized it was his brain. Too many thoughts were running through it. He was worried about everything. He lay there staring up at the ceiling.

"Skyler, Skyler." Came a whisper in the distance.

He heard his name being called. He sat up. "Sam is that you?"

"Yes, can you come help me?"

160

Skyler got out of bed and went to the next room and saw Sam laying there trying to get the covers off. "Skyler could you do me a favor and help me to the bathroom."

"Sure." Skyler went over and helped Sam up. "Do you want me to help you into your chair?"

Sam shook his head. "I can walk a little, just put your arm around me and help me walk to the room. Normally I have my nurse Mark help me. But Michael sent him home for the holidays."

They locked arms around each other, and Skyler helped sam over to the bathroom on the other side of the kitchen. Skyler waited for Sam to be finished and then helped him back to his room. He helped him into bed.

"Thank you, Skyler for being so kind," Sam said as Skyler tucked him in.

"No problem." Skyler let out a long sigh.

"Is there a problem?" Sam asked.

Skyler sat down on the end of the bed. "Kax the girl I like she is pregnant. Well we believe she is. Pregnant and will find out after the holiday. But the thing is, the kid's not mine. I have agreed to pretend it's mine and I'm going to raise it. The thing that bothers me is its half Squallite. I know who the father is, and we can't tell him, and I know nothing about Squallite's. Will it be obvious? Should I raise it with Squallite it's traditions?"

Sam covered his face and shook his head. "First of all, please tell me the father isn't Michael."

Skyler shook his head. He knew he shouldn't say the name, but he had to get it off his chest. "No, it's her friend Jake Mosklin."

Sam let out a long sigh of relief. "Oh good. I know Jake's parents I can understand where she is coming from. Will it be obvious? Probably. The kid might have her ears, but I have seen a few mixed kids in my days and they still usually have their orange eyes. Thick bridged noses, sharp features and they're tall. Unless the kid is a redhead and takes after the mother you will stand out with your blonde hair and green eyes." Sam rubbed his forehead. "But warning

Squallite babies are huge. Michael was 15lbs when he was born, and he was on the small side. Squallite babies are hard to carry even for us. I hope the forces has a good doctor for Kax."

"I hope so too. I have just worried about Kax ever since I found out. And then Nancy threatened her." Skyler put his head into his hands. "I'm trying to help and protect her I have no idea what I'm doing. I don't know how to be a father I know nothing about her and his race. I think I have dug myself into a hole and I won't let myself get out."

Sam put his hand on Skyler's back. "Nobody knows how to be a father the first time. I had to learn everything on my own with Michael. It was not easy I had no job and little money. That's why I joined the forces it was the only way I could get some support. Kax is very lucky to have you. But what were you are saying about this Nancy?"

"Nancy is this girl who I was seeing and things with her got out of hand and well in short she wanted to control me. I told her no, and well she threatened to come after Kax. I haven't told anyone and I'm worried."

Sam paused thinking for a moment. "If my memory is correct Kax did the ritual of On-Mire last year with Jake and Ron right?"

Skyler paused remembering her visiting Jake and Ron weekly and her being in ceremony of Shacog in the Squallite festival over the summer. "Ya I believe that is what she did."

"That makes her an honorary Squallite, and we protect each other. Especially if she is carrying one of our babies. How dangerous do you think Nancy is?" Sam asked.

Skyler rubbed his forehead. "She's very manipulative and-" He didn't want to say it. "She's been able to make me do things that I regretted after."

Sam nodded his head. "You don't have to say anything more. Don't worry about Kax she will be fine."

"Thank you, Sam. I think I can rest easier knowing this." Skyler said standing up. He went back to his bed and was able to sleep.

Chapter 30

Winter holidays were over, and Skyler was back to his regular class schedule. He was on his way to class when he heard and the announcement on the PA, "Cadet Skyler Therris please report to Fleet Admiral Cane's office." He walked down the hall up to Cane's office. Walking in the door, he waved to the secretary and went into the office.

"Hello Skyler, please sit down," Cane said while sitting in his own chair.

Skyler sat down, a little on the reserve around Cane. "So why do you want to see me?"

Cane frowned. "Why the attitude Skyler?"

Skyler groaned. "Because of you I had a horrible holiday, you could have warned me."

Cane puzzled. "What do you mean? I told you to go home because there is a war going on and you hadn't been there for a while what happened?"

Skyler shook his head. "Well you should know my mom is applying for early retirement. It is not because of the war it's because she and Charles are having a baby."

Canes gripped his chest. "What! At her age with him! Why after all this time?"

Skyler sat back and nodded. "Ya, I know I had the same reaction. I got into a fight with her about it and she doesn't want me around anymore and wished me well on the frontlines."

Cane pulled out a bottle of brandy out of his desk and poured him and Skyler a glass. "As long as I'm alive, I will not send you to the front. I try not to send anyone who it isn't necessary. If people aren't ready for the front, then you might as well kill them before they take off. I'm really sorry you had a bad time there, that was not my intentions."

Skyler took a sip out of his glass. "Ya, well she doesn't, believe me Charles is abusive and hates me. I tell you one thing I will not be voting for him when he runs for president."

"He's wants to be president?" Canes eye widened and examined Skyler a bit closer. "Is that where you got that mark?"

Skyler pointed to the remains of the bruise on his cheek. "Ya, he threatened to shoot me if I came back. I spent the first night there and well it all happened all over again. He is nice in front of my mother. He has her duped into thinking what he wants, like all his other supporters in the political world."

"Some days your mother just amazes me," Cane finished his drink and covered his face. "Another thing I want to congratulate you on becoming a father."

Skyler sipped his drink in his cup. "What? When did I become a father?" *How does he know about Kax?*

Puzzled Cane frowned at Skyler. "Didn't Kax tell you about the baby?"

Oh, Kax must have told him. Skyler choked. "Kax isn't letting me say much until we get it confirmed next week."

Cane picked up a file off his desk and handed it to Skyler. "Your father would be so happy. He always loved kids and wanted so many. |He would be happy to know he was going to be a grandfather and his name would live on."

Skyler opened the file. "Uh Cane what is all this paperwork for? We haven't gotten it confirmed yet she might not be pregnant."

"You are aware Kax is going for deep space piloting training. These are all your set of papers that need to be filled out. If you are going to be the father and take responsibility without being married."

A sharp pain went through Skyler's chest. *Cane really believes this child is mine. I haven't even touched Kax. It was one thing being there for her and babysitting but making it official on paper*' He flipped through the papers. He looked up at Cane. "The child is-"

"Skyler you can take this home and look them over. They don't have to be filled out today. Especially since you haven't gotten it confirmed." Cane poured himself another glass. "I always thought you would be older and there wouldn't be a war going on."

"Cane I don't know what to say." He closed the folder and placed it on his lap.

"Don't say anything. This is a confusing and difficult time for both of us." Cane downed his drink. "I'm happy for you Skyler but I think I need to be alone. Sorry."

Skyler left the office and was making his way down towards his next class he heard a deep voice behind him.

Chapter 31

Skyler was sitting in the examination room next to Kax, waiting for the specialist. *This is it.*

A tall dark red haired Catillion wearing a doctor's coat entered the room. "Hello, I am Dr. Cornwall you must be Mr. and Mrs. Therris."

Skyler and Kax choked.

"Were not married, he's just the father," Kax said laying on the table with her belly hanging out waiting for her ultrasound.

"Oh, I'm so sorry about that. There must be a mistake on the paperwork." Dr. Cornwall said.

I all this talk about marriage, do we really need to get married? Skyler held her hand. *Oh, Kax I hope you're not pregnant. I'll be there for the baby, but I really don't want my kid to be the same age as my mother's.*

Laying on the bed Kax squeezed Skyler's hand tighter. This was the moment They had been waiting for.

"It's good the see the nurse already prepped you. Mind if we just get started?" Dr. Cornwall sat down in the rolling chair next to Kax.

"That would be great!" Skyler blurted out.

The doctor laughed at his enthusiasm. "I guess you two are anxious to know." She grabbed a bottle of gel and poured some onto Kax's belly. And took out a wand and started going over her tummy.

"Um, she's a Catillion why are you giving her a human ultrasound?" Skyler asked.

"It's not. This wand reads the insides differently. We right now are checking to see what uterus the child is in. or if there is anything else that could be causing these symptoms." She turned to Kax. "Have your symptoms changed since you last saw Dr. Kelley."

She tensed up with the cold gel on her body. "Yes, I'm not getting morning sickness I have been a bit moody and I have been getting cramps."

The doctor looked at the screen trying to find something. They all watched the screen carefully. After about three minutes of looking around. She held the wand right near her bladder, "According to the paperwork you said you have been pregnant for two months? And the baby is a Squallite but-" She pointed to Skyler. "-you do know he is human?"

Kax nodded. "He's the father but not biological."

"Understood. You do realize, Squallite's carry their babies for twelve months and they are between 15-25lbs. If this was a Squallite we would have to find out when the best time to induce because it couldn't be carried to full term." She moved the wand a bit more. "But I'm seeing engorging and swelling but no signs of a baby anywhere. I could keep checking but I think it's something different. Before this when was the last time you had sex?"

Kax took a moment to think about it. "When I was in high school. Around prom. That would have been 4 years ago."

How does anyone go that long without sex? I didn't even go all of winter holidays without, it was a hard few days, but I was able to bang Michael's neighbor." Skyler gripped his chest. "What about Rantra I thought you and him?"

Kax groaned. "Ew, just when I thought you were growing up. People can go a lot longer without sex. Me and Rantra just did things we never actually had penetrative sex."

"But that's the best part," Skyler added.

"Ahem." The doctor cleared her throat.

They stopped to look at her.

"I need to run a quick blood test on Kax because I think I found the issue." The doctor added. "I need you to hold out your arm."

Kax held out her arm and the doctor took a small silver tube and pressed it on Kax's arm. She took the tube away and stared at it for a moment.

"Well doc is she pregnant?" Skyler asked sitting on the edge of his seat. His hand crushing Kax's.

"I'm afraid not." The doctor shook the tube.

Skyler and Kax both let out a sigh of relief.

"But I'm afraid you have a condition called Felionititus. It's rare but causes a Catillion to go into a pseudopregnancy when she has a major change in her hormones. So, having sex for the first time in a long time probably triggered it."

"See, Kax, I told you to get laid more," Skyler commented.

"STOP IT NOW! Skyler or I will ask you to leave the room!" Kax snapped.

"I'm sorry, Kax." Skyler could see the tears forming in her eyes. He turned to look at the doctor. "Please go on."

"Felionititus doesn't just cause pseudopregnancies it also causes fertility issues making it harder to conceive. Hard to carry a child and limits the number of babies one can have at one time."

Kax held her belly and began to curl up.

"What do you mean limits the number of babies? Are you saying Kax can't have children?" Skyler asked.

"Catillion's have on average 3-5 babies at one time. With Kax's condition, she might have between 1-3 and the babies may not make it. It's going to be really hard for her to have children but not impossible."

Skyler leaned over and gave Kax a hug.

"Be thankful the child wasn't a Squallite baby. Most Catillion's have problems carrying them. But one with your condition would have had a very hard time."

Kax's crying was getting worse.

"I'm going to prescribe a birth control that should help elevate the hormones. Your Pregnancy symptoms should start to fade soon." The doctor got up and handed Skyler her card. "If any of you have any questions feel free to contact me. I'll leave you two alone. Take as much time as you need."

Skyler picked up Kax's chin and smiled at her. "Come on let's get you cleaned up and I will take you home you need rest." Skyler helped Kax with her clothes and walked with her out of the room.

***

Kax walked slowly up the stairs. She was crying and finding it hard to move. But she knew she needed to be somewhere to rest.

Skyler had his arm around her and slowly helped her up the stairs to her room.

Kax began to take her uniform off.

Skyler turned back towards the door.

"Please stay, Skyler. Come to bed and just hold me I don't want to be left alone right now." Kax cried.

"In that case one moment." He left and quickly came back wearing his green issues sweatpants. He got into bed with Kax.

She rolled over and nuzzled herself into his arms. "Are you happy that there isn't a baby?"

Skyler shook his head. "Relieved yes. But it didn't matter to me if there was a baby or not. I was going to take care of you. I'm sorry you got this worse news. But at least you know now."

"It's hard to explain. No, I didn't want this kid now but now I'm going to have a hard time with this in the future." Tears began to roll down her face. "Skyler what am I going to do?"

Skyler held her close wiping the tears off her face. "Take your medication. Stick to it to make things easier and be the best pilot you can be. When you're ready for kids just go to the doctor and talk about plans for them."

"Skyler did you really want this kid or were you trying to get close to me?" She stared up at him with her big sad eyes.

He took a deep breath. "I always believe in doing the right thing. You were going to be a mother without a father and needed support. You're a good friend. I could not let you do it alone. I don't know the first thing about babies, but I was willing to figure it out. I care about you, Kax, and I will take care of you." He gave her a kiss on the top of her head. "But I'm really glad I'm not going to be a father the same year my brother is born."

She pushed away. "What? What brother?"

Skyler sighed. "Over the winter holidays, my mother told me her and Charles are having a baby. They know it is a boy. I'm ignoring her. That's the reason she wanted me back so badly. I'm really glad I'm not becoming a father the same year as Charles."

Kax gave Skyler a hug. "Isn't it weird your mother having a kid when you're old enough to have one yourself?" She yawned.

"Precisely why she is too old." Skyler started to close his eyes. "I love you Kax." He said before he drifted off.

Chapter 32

Skyler rushed down the hall. He didn't want to be late for O'Brien's. Rushing down the hall the bell rang just before he got there. He walked into the class anyway.

O'Brien turned and looked at Skyler. "I will see you in a few minutes you wait outside of the classroom."

This was it, He thought. *I'm in trouble and I am not going to be able to live this one down.* He waited outside for a few minutes.

O'Brien came walking out all looked at Skyler. "Is Kax really pregnant?"

Skyler's eyes widened. "No, we went to the doctor's yesterday. Why are you asking me not her?"

"I was going to but she didn't show up for class. And the file said you were the father so I thought I would confirm with you." O'Brien stated. "When did you and Kax hook up?"

Skyler's heart began to race. "Long story, but what do you mean Kax isn't here? We drove to school together."

"Well she is not in the room. Maybe she went to go do something and is also running late." O'Brien paused. "But I got good news for you. Your request was approved you are going to spend next year on Catillion. Congratulations."

If Kax isn't in class something's wrong, she is never late. His hands began to tremble. "Thanks a lot, sir. That's good news. I got to go." Skyler tried to take off, but O'Brien grabbed his shoulder.

"Where do you think you are going, class is in there." O'Brien pointed.

"Sorry sir but if Kax isn't in that class I have to go find her." Skyler bolted off down the hall. *Where could she be? I have no idea where to start looking. I hope Nancy didn't get her.* He stopped for a second. *Think, Skyler, think. When did you last see her?* "At the car, she said she was going to class and I went to talk to Miri about plans for the weekend." *Anything could have happened to her.* He stood there for a moment thinking of placing on base she could have gone.

"Hey Skyler, what's wrong? you look out worried." Rob's voice came from behind him.

Skyler jerked around and smiled. "Rob am I glad to see you. Kax is missing and I don't know where to look for her. I'm worried."

"Because of Nancy, right?" Rob held up his finger. "I have an idea. I want you to go check Jake's room first she might be there. I'll go look for her on my own."

"Okay I'll do that. Wait how do you know about Nancy and Jake?" Skyler asked.

Rob smirked. "I know things. Now go."

Skyler nodded and ran through the halls to the officers' quarters. He knew Jake's room number only because he saw Kax write it down once. He got to the door. "I hope I remembered it right." He knocked on the door.

Jake opened the door. "Skyler, what are you doing here?"

172

Out of breath Skyler managed to form the words. "Is Kax here?"

Jake was standing in the doorway with sore eyes, messy hair and in his boxers. "No, why would you think she was?"

"She didn't show up for class and I'm worried. I think Nancy might have done something." Skyler said with his heart racing.

Jake stepped aside from the door. "Come in we will talk."

Skyler entered the room and sat down at the little table. "This is what the officers' quarters look like?"

"The Squallite ones. There are nicer ones." He put on a pot of tea. "Do you want some tea?"

"If you got blueberry tea that would be great," Skyler said.

Jake pointed to the kettle. "I mean steeped tea, not cocktails. I don't drink, it screws with my medication." Jake poured a cup for himself and sat down across the table from Skyler. "So, we finally meet."

Skyler stared back at him. "I guess this is a first. Kax has talked about you a lot."

Jake sipped his tea. "Same with you. Now why are you worried about Kax?"

"Because one, she wasn't in class and we came to school together and she's never late, two Nancy threatened to hurt her-"

Jake cut him off. "I know about Nancy from the Squallite grapevine. You came to my room for another reason what was it?"

"I came here because Rob told me to look here," Skyler answered.

"And?" Jake narrowed his eyes. "There is a reason you didn't just run off when I told you she wasn't here."

He's right, I want to know more about this man Kax has fallen for. This man who could have been her baby daddy. What does Kax see in this man? Skyler let out a sigh of defeat. "I guess I was just curious about who you were."

Jake nodded. "It's very understandable." He was quiet for a moment then asked. "I'm going on a rumor but was the baby mine?"

Skyler's heart stopped. "I'm not supposed to say."

Jake waved his hand. "It's fine I won't tell her I know. And she made the right choice. I'm in a very bad place right now in my life I would be the worst parent. And a child that mixed has its best chance trying to pass as human on this planet. I'll be distancing myself from Kax in the next little bit. You have nothing to fear from me."

"Okay fine. What about Nancy? Do you think Nancy has Kax?" Skyler narrowed his eyes.

"I'm going to say just two things about Nancy, be more cautious about the people you fuck. Maybe get to know them and stop picking up random sluts. Also, if Nancy has her, Rob's already got everything under control. Before you ask, I know Rob. Probably why he sent you here."

He's right I caused this. Any harm that comes to Kax is my fault. A tear came to Skyler's eye. "I never wanted to hurt Kax. I love her."

"We all love her, in one way or another."

There was a knock at the door. Jake got up and opened the door. Kax stood there panting. "Hey, Jake, is Skyler here."

Jake stepped aside and pointed.

Skyler stood up. Kax had a tear on the shoulder of her uniform. "Kax are you okay?" His heart was pounding.

She ran into his arms. "It was awful. I was heading to class. When Nancy came up to me, she started talking all friendly and then she asked me to go to her room with her. I said no. she grabbed me and started pulling me. I tried to fight her off but she was so strong. She tried to take me to her room and then Rob showed up. Oh my gosh, he was scary. His eyes were so black. He pinned Nancy against the wall and started choking her because she wouldn't let me go. When I got free, he told me where to find you. I don't know anything after that. Skyler, what is going on?"

Skyler held Kax close. "Nancy has been threating me. I ignored her and well now my friends are suffering I'm so, very sorry."

Jake scoffed. "I think it is time you sat down and told Kax the entire story."

Skyler nodded. "Yes, let me explain."

Chapter 33

Michael was in his room studying hard. Exams were tomorrow, and he was worried about failing. He might have slacked off during the years, but he knew failing an exam would mean he would lose the whole course. Commodore gray's class was the hardest to study for. The man was so unpredictable who knew what the exam would be on. They covered a little bit of everything he could choose any number of subjects for them to write about. When that man had a plan you never knew what to expect.

It was late into the night. Michael had already planned to just stay up for the entire night studying and then taking the exam in the morning. The study hall was empty. *I wonder if I am in the wrong place why isn't anyone else here?* He thought.

"That's the wrong textbook." Rob's voice said from behind Michael.

Michael jerked around in his seat. "Rob, what are you doing here? And how do you know? Grey just told us to study everything."

Rob pulled out the seat next to Michael. "When has Grey ever told us the right thing to do. I took his exam last year. He gets you to read everything possible when he is going to just give you a freelance exam. When you must invent or create a new theory. He wants to see what creative minds we have when we're under stress. And from what I have seen of your work you're going to pass."

Michael rubbed his face. "Why should I believe you?"

Rob smiled. "Because as much as you and your friends don't trust me, I have never lied to any of you. Unlike Grey who has almost never given you a straight answer."

He does have a point. "Fine then, I will take your advice and put the books away. Now since were alone can I ask you some personal questions?"

Rob laughed. "Were in the research library of the unexplained, we're not alone. Put the books away and come to my room."

Michael scanned around the room. "There is nobody here."

Rob took one of the engineering textbooks on alien engineering and open it to one of the back pages. On the page was a black disk. He pressed a few of the colored bottoms. "We are not alone." He spoke into the disk. Rob's words were repeated throughout the collection coming from different books. "See if could use this disk as speaker what else do you think I can do with the stuff in these books?"

Michael's eyes were wide with amazement. "Wow, okay you win. Let us go to your room."

Rob gave him a devilish grin.

Rob's room had only one bed and the sheets were black. There was a desk and it was smaller than a standard dorm room. "How did you get a whole room to yourself?" Michael asked.

"By being put on the dangerous persons list," Rob said siting down on his bed. "Now what questions would you like to ask."

"Well it is been something I have been wondering. When you said you have killed before who was it? And what is your connection to the Squallite's, I have never heard of you?" Michael took a seat at Rob's desk.

"I knew you were going to ask this eventually. It all began when I was a child, my dad was a hard worker and always working even when he was at home and he needed absolute silence. If me or my brother and sister made noise while he worked, he would beat us. He was very ruthless. Finally, one day when I was 7 my little sister was 5 and my bother who was 8 were outside on balcony. We often when outside when my dad was working to reduce the volume in the house. My sister kept making a big fuss in fear of my dad beating us I grabbed a seat cushion and covered her face. When she didn't wake up, I didn't understand to cover up what I had done I pushed her off the balcony and told everyone we were playing, and she fell. As I got older, I developed my dad's attitude for quietness so I would go out to the barn and work. It just held hay and stuff no animals besides for some cats. The cats were cute and friendly I enjoyed their company until one of them had kittens. The noise from the crying kittens bothered me and I would lash out and kill the kittens. It gave me a release from the pain. Over time I just started killing them to feel in control and give me the stress release. It wasn't until I was in my first year of university when I came back for the holidays, my brother brought his wife and child. I was trying to study, and my dad was retired by then but sometimes still did work on some projects. I asked everyone to be quiet, but it turned into a fight. In my rage I killed them all. That's not what the courts think. I told them my dad killed them and I killed him in self defense. The courts believed it I was analyzed and that's where I met Commodore Grey. He was working with the university at the time and saw my research and to keep me out of jail I agreed to be sent to Squall and go for meditation therapy with the order of Scarik while continuing my research. Once I earned their trust, I was able to return to earth with my research. Commodore Grey keeps an eye on me."

Michael stared at him in shock. "Wow, I never thought the story was that…"

"Messed up. Yes, I know. I have a few wires that don't quite work in my brain. That is my main research project finding a way to fix my brain. I'm not a medical scientist but I'm a chemical engineer. That's why I work with Perry because I find sources of chemical for his plants. I'm trying to figure out what is wrong with my brain and balance the chemical correctly. I come up with formula's find sources and supply them to the doctors who make them into pills and see how things go. I haven't cured myself, but I have helped others." Rob sat there staring a Michael. "So, any more questions?"

Michael's stomach was beginning to flip. "No, I think you answered all of them."

Rob let out a sigh. "Michael, I know this might make you feel uneasy, but I'm trying. I have improved so much. I never have tantrums anymore. Used to have them all the time. I'm on your side. I'm one of the good guys. I also have come to a balance between studying and killing people. I know when and where to study so that I'm not near anyone. Are you okay with this?"

Michael hesitantly replied. "You just told me you slaughtered your entire family for being noisy. Skyler would not have survived a week being your roommate. Heck, most of the people I know would not have. Why should I trust you after all of this?"

For the first time, Michael could see the color in Rob's eyes and not just black dots. They were greyish blue. "Because the Squallite's trust me and have accepted me they saw the change and they have seen the improvement in me. They know I'm not fine but have faith in me. They took me under their wing and," He rolled up his sleeve to reveal an orange bird tattoo on his left forearm. "I think you know what this means."

Michael looked closely at the tattoo. "I have only seen that once before when I was kid one summer on squall. My dad told me to stay away from him and explained that tattoo meant you belong to the Squallite's. You committed a horrible crime against your own kind, but we took you in. You are not one of us but you're like our foster child and we protect you as long as you do not break our laws."

Rob nodded. "They gave it to me after years of work. The other guy you saw when you were a kid was probably Josh Comets, he is further along than me. Last I heard he was on Virgo 5 he didn't go into the forces he became a Squallite monk."

Michael sighed. "So now what. I know your story. I have exams in four hours what do I do you said not to study."

Rob patted the bed. "If you want, we can crash together. I know you Squallites just go into the meditative trance and don't sleep so you'll be alert if I do try to kill you."

Michael's eyes widened. "Ugh."

Rob laughed. "that was a bit of dark humor sorry about that. You could meditate in the chair. I know there is no point in you driving home back right now. I can sleep on top of the covers if you like."

Michael pondered the offer for a few moments. "I will share the bed I will lay on top of the covers and you can enjoy the blanket."

Rob nodded his head. "Sounds like a plan. Rest well."

Chapter 34

Skyler sat on the couch waiting for Kax to finish in the kitchen. "Kax, are you done with the dishes, yet I want to watch a movie with you."

She groaned, "I will be done when I'm done!"

Skyler looked over at Michael who was sitting in the living chair looking at his tablet. "Hey, Mike I was wondering what you think the Cass are after?"

Michael looked up at Skyler. "Do not call me Mike that's not my name. And why do you think the Cass want something: other than kill us?"

Skyler moved to the edge of the couch next to Michael. "Well think about it they're attacking only Earth and a few Squall places but nowhere else. And they're not killing as many as they could be there just attacking specific spots almost like they want something."

Michael thought about it for a minute. "You might be on to something but besides that orb, I do not know any other connection between Earth the Cass and Squall."

"Well, the Cass might not be the angry bloodthirsty demons we think they are. I know they look like demons with the horns but maybe here is another reason for starting this war other than hate?"

Michael typed a few things into his tablet. "The first war with them was because they were an angry primitive warlord race that wanted to invade Earth. That is what I was taught and no one else has said differently. This time, I guess maybe they just want to do the same thing and kill the positions off so then we will have no leaders."

Skyler shook his head. "I don't even believe that garbage their race is not primitive they were advanced. They know what they're doing, there's a cover-up going on."

Michael nodded. "I agree with you, but I do not know who out there will tell us the truth, this seems like something that has been buried deep."

Kax entered the living room and sat on the couch. "Sounds like Earth screwed up and someone said let's deal with it by covering up the whole thing. Sounds like an Earth thing to do."

Skyler and Michael shot Kax a dirty look.

Kax leaned back on the couch. "Sorry, right, you two are Earth lovers. Don't get me wrong I love Earth too, but it is run by humans who even though have men and women running this planet are still arrogant. It doesn't matter if you have a man or women running things, they all think like the same because now they're politicians. Those leaders of yours screwed up and not they will not admit it."

Skyler listened to what Kax had to say. "Well then what do you think we do about this?"

Kax smiled. "Well first we will talk to a few people, ask around and see what we can find out. Ask Cane, Commodore Grey, Davis, Justin and you're going to hate me for this Charles."

Skyler's eyes widened. "You want me to talk to Charles the man who wants me dead, no I will not talk to him."

Michael cuts in. "What does Grey have to do with this?"

Kax sighed. "Skyler if you don't want to talk to Charles I will talk to him he hasn't met me yet. And Grey because he is a Squallite with a job no other Squallite has. He knows more than it may seem."

Skyler laughed. "I'll talk to Charles, if you talk to him my mother might want to kill you. And why my uncle Justin?"

She nodded. "Well not really him but his connections he talks to the King or people close to the King. We are still not sure what side this cover up coming from just that it is Earth and one of the leaders, president or kings caused it. Do you think we can do it?"

Michael shook his head. "I do think we can do it, but we are walking down a dangerous path. If there really is a cover-up, then this is the kind of thing where we can be killed in an 'accident.'"

Kax agreed. "I'm willing to take that risk. And I think we should get Rob in on this because it is so dangerous."

Skyler looked confused. "Why Rob?"

"Because of what I have seen and what Michael told us about Rob then he is the type of guy to know how to get things done or issue a few accidents if it comes down to that." She smugly said.

"No one is having any accidents." Skyler narrowed his eyes at Kax. "Even if Rob has killed that is no reason to make him kill again."

Michael nodded his head. "Skyler is right. I do not think we should consider death. If we are getting into something that can get us, we should walk away now."

Kax signed. "Fine, if this gets too dangerous, we get out as fast as we can."

Skyler turned to look at the TV and grabbed the remote. "Come on now let's clear our minds and watch a movie."

Chapter 35

Kax knocked on the archway of the hospital door. Jake was holding Ron's hand in the hospital bed. His eyes were full of tears, his face was red and sore like he had not slept in days and had been crying the entire time.

Jake lifted his head and looked towards Kax. "Thank you for coming please sit down."

Kax entered the room and took the chair next to Jake. "How is he doing?"

Jake wiped the flood of tears off his face. "He comes in and out of consciousness. The doctors are trying to slow the infection at this point, but it isn't doing much. His body is slowly shutting down. Thank you for coming. I believe this is the end."

Ron squeezed Jake's hand and opened his swollen eyes. "Kax are you there?"

Kax leaned closer and placed her hand on Ron's arm. "Yes, I'm here."

Ron let out a groan of pain. "Thank you for coming." He coughed. "You've been a good friend I'm glad to have you by my side." He rolled his head over to his side. "Jake I'm afraid my time is at an end. Please remember me as a human. If anyone asks, I was human. That's all I ever wanted was to live and die as a human. But I'm glad to die surrounded by the company of friends." He continued to cough and cough. Finally, he whispered the word "Elgastinic." And closed his eyes one last time.

Jake gripped Ron's hand harder and shook his arm. He got up from his chair in a panic and shook Ron. "Please don't go. Please wake up." The tears were pouring off his face. "I love you. You can't leave me!" Jake laid his head on Ron's chest. "Please don't leave me."

The nurse and the doctor entered the room. They brought a defibrillator and a syringe of some clear liquid. The nurse injected the syringe into Ron's arm.

"Jake please get off the patient." The doctor said.

"No, no. I can't let go. He has to live!" Jake cried hugging the body.

Kax grabbed Jake's shoulders trying to pull him off. "Jake you have to let him go. The doctor is trying to save his life!"

Jake conceded and loosened his grip. He didn't say anything and just ran out the door.

Kax stayed and watched the medical staff try desperately to bring Ron back to life. They tried and tried but nothing would work. Tears came to Kax's eyes as the doctor called the time of death. The doctor turned to Kax. "Are you family?"

Kax shook her head. "No, but Jake was his partner."

"Well if you can get him back here, we need him or a family member to fill out some paperwork." The doctor said.

Kax nodded her head. She had to get Jake back there and get him to fill out Ron's paperwork before Ron's parents showed up. "I'll go get him." She rushed down the hall. Trying to figure out where Jake went. She finally found him at the end of the hall curled up into a small alcove between the elevator and the wall. She stood in front of the alcove. "Jake you have to go and fill out some paperwork."

Jake shook his head. "No! It's a lie he can't die. Please don't make me go back there. I can't bear it!"

Kax sat down the floor in front of him. "Jake I'm so sorry but you can't change what is done. At least he isn't suffering now."

"No, he's not suffering, but he left me behind on this planet to suffer." Jake cried into his knees. "Why did he leave me?"

Kax shook her head. "I don't think he wanted to. He fought to stay alive for you. You know that's true."

Jake stared at Kax with his bloodshot orange eyes, they had been to sore to wear his blue contacts. "Kax do you know what elgastinic means?"

Kax shook her head. "I don't know that squall word."

"It means, it is time to die. It's a Squallite goodbye." He covered his face. "He's gone forever, and I don't know how I can go on."

Kax placed her hand on Jake's knee. "I don't know but what I do know is if you don't claim the body before his parents arrive, you're going to lose him forever."

Jake's eye's popped. "Shit they better not call his parents. Not right now. Ron wasn't on good terms with them." He jumped to his feet. "They will have no say in his death. They never wanted to have anything to do with him once he told them about his change."

Kax got up and moved out of the way for Jake to get up.

Jake rushed back to the hospital room. The Nurse was cleaning the room. "Where is the paperwork I fill out?"

The nurse looked up from the bed she was making. "Go to the nurse's station."

Jake left the room across the hall to the nurse's station. "Hello I'm Jake Mosklin, Ron Kernic's partner."

She handed him a digital clipboard. "Here you go fill this out."

Jake took the clipboard and sat down on a seat nearby.

Kax soon joined him as he filled out the paperwork. "Do you have plans for the funeral?"

Jake's heart sank. "I never thought of it. Ron never mentioned one. I could host one, but I don't know if it would be worth the cost if less than ten people go. I don't want a funeral with the forces. They give you such a generic grave and I know a lot of people would be annoyed because of his life choices." He began to fill out the form.

Kax put her hand on Jake's shoulder. "Might I make a suggestion?"

"I'm listening." He said not taking his eyes off the clipboard.

"My friends Michael and Perry are working on a top-secret plant that could help us in the war. I don't know the full details, but I know they are keeping a lot of it top secret. But I know they need a chemical that high amounts are found in Squallite and Catillion bodies. If you don't want a funeral would you consider donating Ron's body for this research?"

Jake slowly turning his head towards Kax and glared at her. "Donate a body? You know that is against Squallite tradition. How could you think to ask me that?"

Knowing she asked a seriously taboo question she didn't back down. "You're not a Squallite remember? You two have broken every other Squallite rule what's the problem with one more?"

"Squallite bodies must remain intact after death." He snapped.

"Ron wasn't a Squallite!" Kax snapped back.

Tears came to Jake's eyes. "You're right, how could I forget that?"

Kax put her hand on Jake's back and rubbed it. She heard the BING of the elevator. She saw an older Squallite couple get off. She tapped Jake on the shoulder. "Um I don't know how they got here this fast. But is that Ron's parents?"

Jake's eyes widened, and he grabbed Kax's shoulder. "They probably transported here, they also work on base. Stall them until I get this paperwork done. I don't care what you do. They hate me."

Kax nodded and got out of the seat and went over the aging couple. *I have no idea what to say to them. If I don't mention Ron what can I do? Here goes nothing.* She ran up to them. "Hi there, are you here to visit anyone?"

Ron's father had white streaks in his hair. "What does it matter to you?"

"Well if you are, I notice you have no gifts in your hands. I thought you should know the hospital is offering a limited time promotion. A free $50-dollar gift card for the gift shop. Would you like me to escort you to the gift shop?"

Ron's mother glared at her with her orange eyes. It was shocking how much she looked like Ron. Her hair was a lighter brown than Ron's, but the facial features matched. But it was clear from his frown he was his father. "Our son is dead! We don't need any gift and who gives that job to a pilot?"

Kax's ears folded. She had forgotten that she was still in her uniform. "Oh no that's so sad. What was his name? What was his age?"

The father glared. "Move aside and let us continue on our way."

186

Kax was frozen she had no idea what to do now. She felt a tap on her shoulder. She jerked her head to see Jake standing next to her.

Jake whispered into her ear. "Thanks, I'll take it from here. I sent you a text."

"You have no right to be here!" Ron's father snapped.

Kax nodded and bolted towards the elevators. As she waited for the elevator. She could hear shouts of things like. "You're the reason he's dead." "You put these crazy ideas into his head." She didn't stay to listen she got on the elevator and checked her messages. In the elevator, she read the text. *Hey Kax, thanks for your help and support. Let your friend Michael know I'm having the body sent to science for him. I'll be in touch this is for the future no point in staying in the past. -Jake.* Kax smiled with glee she could not wait to tell Michael.

Chapter 36

Perry, Michael, Rob, Grey and Jake stood over the body of Ron laying on the cold slab in the morgue. The body had been flash-frozen to preserve the body before any decay.

"I do not like this idea," Michael said. He looked around to see everyone's reaction.

"I agree, Michael, but you need the chemicals and he has the amount you need. His body should go to some use." Jake said.

"I'm just glad we were able to get a donated body," Rob added.

Michael shot Rob a suspicious look. "Maybe we should just burry the body."

Perry put his arms over the glass frozen tomb. "No! We need this body. Do you know how long and hard I have been working on these plants? I have tried so many alternatives this is the only way it will work."

"Is that why your skin is purple?" Grey asked.

"Neptunian plums. I'm on a diet of them and potatoes with this new batch of plants. The plums have high amounts of violetiod and turn your skin purple. If we get this body, I can go off this diet and return to my regular color." Perry pleaded.

Rob laughed. "Purple Perry I like it."

"The body has already been donated to us. It's going to be used. Jake is the only one who can change his mind about this now." Grey pointed out.

All eyes were on Jake. "I might have made the choice a bit quickly, but I have thought about it. The Squallite's will only take him if he is a Squallite and Earth is too expensive to bury him. I could only afford cremation. So, I might as well send his body to be used. My only request is if I could keep a part of his body?" Jake requested.

Grey leaned his head. "It's not useable after death you know that right."

Groans came from the crowd.

Jake covered his mouth and tried not to laugh. "Not that part. I don't care if it is a finger or a toe, even an ear would be ok."

Rob nodded. "No problem." He went over to the drawers on the other side of the morgue and looked for a jar. He found one in the bottom drawer. He then went over the lab table and grabbed a bottle of red liquid and a syringe. When he had gathered all the supplies, he opened the frozen tomb.

They all coughed at the icy smoke that filled the room. Rob was able to snap Ron's right ring finger off. He held it up with his wedding band still attached. "Is this good enough?"

Jake coughed. "Yeah that's fine but I didn't need it now."

Rob closed the tomb and the mist turned to condensation. "It has to be now. Because when this meeting is done the body's going to the grinder." Rob placed the finger on a small table on the side. He filled the syringe and then injected the liquid into the finger before putting it in the jar. He sealed the jar and handed it to Jake. "Here you go."

Jake looked at the severed finger. "What did you do to it?"

"I injected it with a chemical that will prevent it from ever decaying. You can make it into a necklace if you want to now."

Jake stared at the finger. "Um, thank you."

"So, are we all good? Are we done talking?" Rob asked anxiously.

All eyes were on Jake. A tear came to Jake's eyes. "Can I have one last goodbye? Then you can do whatever is necessary."

They all nodded and left Jake alone in the room.

Chapter 37

Skyler was sitting at the kitchen table across from Michael. They had their books spread out over the table. The books were open, and Skyler was staring blankly at the pages.

"Skyler your reading a book? I'm surprised." Kax said as she entered the room.

He looked up from his textbook. "Michael made me. You had the keys and he wouldn't lend me his."

Kax sat down at the table with the boys. She shifted the books around checking to see which ones they were reading. "Well exams are soon. You should be studying."

"I feel like we just had exams. This last semester just flew by." He groaned.

Kax turned her focus towards Michael. "How long has he been working?"

Michael raised his head from his book. "About an hour, why does it matter?"

"Well I'm back I could give him the car now?" Kax suggested.

Skyler shook his head. "No point. Miri and Perry will be here soon. Michael and Perry have a project they are working on. And Miri is staying the night."

Kax's eyes widened. "Who said you could have girls over, we didn't agree to this."

Skyler closed his book and turned towards Kax. "Who said you could bring a guy over? We never really talked about it I know. But we didn't say no to it. Look if it bothers you, I will take her out somewhere now that we have a vehicle, but I don't see what the big deal is?"

Kax's eyes became red and she was holding back the hurt. "Fine whatever bring her over, what do I care." She rushed off.

Skyler rushed after her. "Kax let's talk about this!"

She went upstairs to her room.

Skyler followed behind her. He knocked on her door. "Kax please talk to me. We can work something out."

"Skyler, you're a jerk. Go away," Kax called out.

"You know I can't go away. Because I need to know what to do about Miri?" he said.

"Fine open the door and you can come in and talk," Kax said.

He did just that. He didn't sit on the bed instead just stood by the door in case she told him to leave again. "So, what's the problem? Why are you upset?"

Kax looked up from her pillow she had been crying into. "I know you own this house. I know we're not together. It's just this is my childhood home and I don't want to hear you make love to another woman."

Skyler scoffed, "It's not making love when me and Miri do it. She has a boyfriend. They have an agreement and we are reliable hookups is all. Kax if it is the noise we can go to the basement and try to be quiet. Or if it is because it's your childhood home, I will just go somewhere else with her. I'm willing to make this work."

Kax stared at Skyler with her teary eyes. "No, she can stay. I'm sorry I got so upset."

Skyler went over and sat on the bed. "Kax you're still upset. Is it something to do with me seeing other women? I know we're not a couple, but we did start to bond with the baby."

Kax leaned over and nuzzled next to Skyler and he wrapped his arm around her. "Skyler in the last little while our lives have been spun in a circle. I don't know how to feel about anything anymore. I know it was just a shock. I don't know why but I didn't expect it."

He rubbed Kax's shoulder. "This changes nothing between us. I still care about you. But we're not a couple unless that's what you want to be?"

Kax pushed away from Skyler. "Go have your date! And do whatever you want just to keep it in your room. You're right, you're not my boyfriend."

Skyler got up off the bed. Feeling confused and worried. "Is this a side effect from the new medication? I don't know maybe Miri can explain Kax to me."

By the time Skyler had gotten downstairs Perry and Miri were already there. Perry was sitting at the kitchen table with Michael. All their textbooks had been put away and now the table was covered with two laptops linked together. Some test tube samples, and a few plants.

Skyler smelled it as soon as he got into the kitchen. He looked at the counter and saw three pizzas, a container of fries and other various bar snacks. "Perry what's with all the food? I thought you were on a diet of gummy bears or something."

Perry's purple skin was fading to the point where he looked like he was very cold all the time. "Since we got Ron's body donation, I don't need to try different diets and so I can eat what I want. It was Miri's idea to bring food since I told her that me and Michael will be pulling an all nighter for a few days to get these plants germinated. You have an awesome girlfriend by the way Skyler, I like this one."

"That's very nice of you to say Perry." She turned Skyler away from the food and gave him a big kiss. "Miss me?"

"Oh, course I did." Skyler kissed Miri on lips. "Did you bring any drinks?"

Miri reached over and opened the fridge door. There was a 24 case of beer sitting on the shelf. "I couldn't forget."

Skyler put his arm around her and dipped kissed Miri passionately. "You're an amazing woman and you know me so well."

Kax entered the room, clearing her throat.

Skyler stepped back from Miri and brushed himself off. "Hey, Kax, guess what Miri brought, pizza and snacks."

Kax walked over to Miri and held out her hand. "So, your Miri, it is nice to meet you."

Miri smiled taking Kax's hand. "Glad to meet you too. I have heard so much about you. Skyler talks about you all the time."

"Does he now?" Kax went over to the cupboard, grabbed a plate and put a couple of meat lover's pizza slices on it.

Miri whispered into Skyler's ear. "What's up with her?"

"I think she's jealous, I'll explain later," Skyler whispered back

Skyler grabbed a plate of pizza and a couple of beers out of the fridge. "Come on, I'll show you around."

***

Lying in bed naked Skyler kissed Miri on the forehead. She had her arms wrapped around him. "How is it that you always know what I need?"

She looked up towards Skyler. "So, what is going on between you and Kax? Last time I talked to you she found out she was pregnant."

Skyler sighed. "She's not pregnant she has a condition that made her go into a false pregnancy. Since there is no baby, I can tell you it wasn't mine. But I was going to pretend I was the father and raise it with her. But I think she's jealous or something. I don't understand her. She doesn't want to date me but now when I'm going out with a girl or bringing you over, she doesn't like it. When we thought she was pregnant she didn't care, and I was with lots of women. She doesn't make sense."

Miri laid her head on Skyler's chest. "Probably because she was still in denial and not serious. I'll talk to her if you like?"

Skyler let out a long sigh and played with Miri's long blonde wavy hair. "Would you? Believe it or not, I don't have much experience talking to women. And I tried earlier before you showed up and well that didn't work out."

She moved up and kissed Skyler on the lips. "I'll go down and talk to her. You rest up for round two."

Skyler grinned. "Damn, you are amazing."

***

Kax was sitting on the couch eating a sandwich watching the holo-tv.

Miri sat down on the couch next to her. "You do know there is pizza and snacks in the kitchen, right?"

Kax narrowed her eyes at Miri. "I know."

"Kax can we talk for a moment?"

Kax put down her sandwich. "Fine what do you want to talk about?"

"You and Skyler," Miri said. "I want to-"

"Stop right there. There is nothing going on between me and him and he can do whatever he wants because he's Skyler. No responsibility Skyler!"

Miri smiled smugly. "Well from that last statement it sounds like there is something. Kax you can trust me. I want to help you."

Kax stared at Miri for a long time before she said. "Answer me this question first. How can a woman who has a boyfriend run around with a man who is not her boyfriend?"

"I'm not cheating. I'm polyamorous. I have been with my boyfriend since high school. We believe you can love more than just one person equally. We are together but we can see and date other people. He just makes sure I'm safe. He is off planet right now as he is taking his last year on Pluto. He knows about Skyler and the others. He has no issues with it. He has a girlfriend on Pluto. We are still together, and we will be no matter how far apart we are."

Kax looked at her shocked. "Really? You could do that. Aren't you worried he will fall for a woman and love her more?"

Miri shook her head. "Nope I trust him, and I know our bond is strong."

194

Kax just stared at her.

"It's not for everyone. But can I ask you a few questions now?" Miri asked.

Kax paused. "Sure, ask what you want to know."

"What is your issue with Skyler and me or really just Skyler? I doubt this has much to do with me." Miri asked.

I guess I better open up to someone. Kax sighed. "I feel Skyler was just being nice to me because he thought that me being a single mother was his chance to have sex with me. How can he just hop into bed with another woman?"

Miri raised an eyebrow. "Were you together? He told me the baby wasn't his? And you knew about him with other women during this time?"

Kax sighed. "Yes, I knew, and he didn't hide it. We have never had sex the baby wasn't his. It's just when we thought I was pregnant he was different. He was very attentive and caring, women and drinking came second to him. I know I'm not his girlfriend so he's free, but if I was would he be faithful to me? Would he care and would he put me first? Does he even know how to be a proper boyfriend?"

Miri smiled. "I understand. You like him, but you still have your doubts about him. Well I will tell you what I know about Skyler. He is an honorable guy. He knows how to listen to women and cares about making them happy. Their happiness makes him happy. His knowledge about women comes from being with women. Have you ever asked him about his childhood? He didn't really have anyone to tell him what is right or wrong. He's had to figure it out as he went. He might be immature and doesn't have a clue on a lot of subjects, but he has a kind heart and cares, he just needs to get more experience. He's got a lot of potential."

"So, what you're saying is I should give him a chance?" Kax asked.

"If you want to. But he's not going to break your heart. I think he is the type to get his heart broken. He will be a good boyfriend and he will do anything for you. Even if it causes him pain. He's got a lot to learn, he's still a boy."

"But he still runs around with so many women and drinks all the time."

"So, he likes sex who doesn't? He's still young so his drinking will calm down. I bet if you asked him to cut back, he would for you. He's safe and cautious with the women he is with. He really knows how to show a woman a good time." Miri smiled. "Are you feeling better?"

Kax nodded her head. "You have given me lots to think about. Want to join me in watching a movie?"

Miri smiled, "Sure, just let me go get some pizza. Want some?" She got off the couch heading to the kitchen.

"Sure, get me a slice of the meat lovers," Kax said.

Chapter 38

Skyler was walking down the hall heading to class. When he was tapped on the shoulder. He jerked around and saw Cane standing behind him. "Cane what you are doing here?"

Cane had a serious stare on his face. "Follow me we need to talk."

"What about my class?" Skyler asked.

"Don't worry about it. Come with me." Cane said.

Skyler followed Cane. He had no idea where he was taking him. It wasn't to the office that was behind them. Soon they got to a hallway Skyler did recognize. It was the security hallway he went to last year when he and his friends went on there mission to Squall. "Why are we here?"

Cane didn't reply. He just typed in a code to security room 2 and opened the door. "Come with me."

Skyler entered the room behind Cane. "Wha-" A red security officer grabbed Skyler and sat him down in a chair.

"Answer all our questions and you will be okay. Tell us what you know about Nancy and Rob Thorne!" The Security officer shouted at Skyler.

Skyler's hand was shaking. "Uh." Was all he could manage to say.

Cane put his hand on the officer's shoulder. "Stand down. He's just a boy." The officer stepped back, and Cane looked at Skyler. "When was the last time you saw Nancy Marlow."

Painful memories of that last night with Nancy came flooding back into his mind. "Last time I saw her she was trying to get back with me or for me to get her girlfriend back. If I didn't do one or the other, she was going to hurt Kax. That was the last time I saw her. It was before winter holidays."

Cane looked at Skyler. "Did you think of reporting her threat?"

Skyler shook his head. "No, I figured she had no power and just kept an eye on Kax. She did come after Kax after the holidays. Rob found her for me, but I never saw her. Kax told me he had held her against the wall and choked her. But I don't know anything more than that."

"Rob never told you what happened after?" The security officer asked.

Skyler shook his head. "I never asked. Like I mentioned, Nancy and I ended on bad terms and I didn't care to ask or find out. Rob knew this so I don't think he would have cared to tell me. All I care about is she has left me, Ray and Kax alone."

Cane grabbed a chair and sat down in front of Skyler. "What happened with you and Nancy?"

Skyler looked down at his feet. He kicked his feet and twiddled his thumbs. "She was too controlling and things with her got out of hand."

"Did you ever tell Rob about what Nancy did? Did you ever ask him to help you with her?" The officer asked.

Skyler sighed in defeat. "No, I told him about her yes but also I told Perry about her. I didn't say it word for word, but he knew. I never asked for help with her. What are you talking about? What does my relationship with Nancy have to do with anything?"

"Nancy has gone missing. That day with Kax, her and Rob in the hallway was the last time she was seen. We were trying to figure out if you had anything to do with or knew about her disappearance."

Nancy disappeared? No wonder she left me alone. I wonder what happened? Skyler was dumbfounded. "I had no idea…"

"We have talked to everyone else. You were the last one who we needed to get the story from." Cane said.

Skyler shook his head. "I have no idea what happened to her. Sorry I can't help you. Can I go now?"

"One more question Skyler." Cane said. "What did Nancy do to you that could have possibly led to these events?"

I guess I have no choice. Not wanting to admit it he let out a long sigh. "She sexually abused me, and Rey. Please don't make me go into any more details."

The room was silent. The security officer opened the door. "You can go now, cadet."

Chapter 39

Skyler woke up and was making his way down the stairs. His eyes were crusty, and his hair was a mess. He saw Michael packing a suitcase. "You're still here? I thought you would have left in the morning with Kax for exams?"

"I wrote Grey's exam, but I am exempt from the rest of my exams. I have a project to finish and they want me working on this 100% of the time. But good news is we got the plants to germinate correctly and all is going according to plan. They were tested for transportation and they survived so they are sending me to Catillion to work with an expert on finalizing these plants."

Skyler rubbed his face. He brushed his hair back with his hand as he made his way to the fridge. He opened the fridge and grabbed a beer. "So, we can have the kitchen table back again? You and Perry are done with all your experiments?" He opened his can of beer and took a big sip. "I never realized how much we used the table until you took it."

Michael started to clean off the table. "I am sorry about that. We got a little carried away."

Skyler took his beer and sat down at the table. "So how long are you going for?"

Michael took a laser wand out of the kitchen drawer. He turned it on and waved the light over the table and watched as all the dirt disappeared and the table was cleaned. He then put the wand back into the drawer. "Until it is done? I think a year form now." He took a seat across from Skyler.

"So, you're going first. Then, after exams, Kax is going. And I'll be there in fall with Perry unless they change his plans. What about your dad what you going to do about him?" Skyler asked.

"Perry is working on a few other projects," Michael said. "He found a full-time health care worker. He is well enough to work a desk job. He has a cane now and we keep in touch. I have talked to him about leaving and he is encouraging me to go. This will be the longest I have ever been apart from him. I know I have been living here the past year, but you know I go to visit him on weekends and holidays. I cannot do that where I am going. So, no choice."

"It's going to be boring here without you, Skyler said, finishing his beer.

Michael tapped his fingers on the table. "You never are bored for long. You will be fine."

Skyler paused for a moment looking at his empty beer. "Did Cane question you about Nancy's disappearance?"

Michael nodded his head. "He did and I probably know less than you on the subject."

"What do you think happened to her?" Skyler fiddled with the can.

"I do not want to judge or say anything until they find her," Michael said. "But I thin you know what happened."

Skyler let out a sigh. "So, you're all packed? Does that mean you're leaving today?"

Michael nodded. "Yup I was on my way out when you woke up."

"Want me to give you a ride to base?" Skyler offered.

"Kax has the car. You do not need to go to base. I was just going to park my bike at the base." Michael replied.

"That costs money to do that for a year." Skyler stood up. "Give me a few moments I will get dressed and be really nice and park it wherever you want. Either back here or at your dad's place. I don't have an exam till tomorrow evening. Consider it a going away gift."

"Well that is a nice offer. If you take it to my dad's, you will have a long trip back. I would recommend that you just park it in the garage, it is closer."

"Sounds like a plan lets go for one last ride!" Skyler stood up and shot his beer can into the garbage can four feet away.

"You get dressed but I am driving. I want to get there alive and in one piece." Michael said in a stern voice while standing up.

***

When the boys got to the school they were greeted with a surprise. Michael stopped the bike when Skyler tried to stand up when it was still moving.

"Skyler sit down unless you want to get killed, I see it too!" Michael slowed the bike down trying not to jerk Skyler out of it.

In the distance, they could see three security officers taking Rob away. They were guiding him into the back of a police van. When the bike was fully stopped Skyler jumped out and ran towards Rob. Michael followed behind him.

"Hey, what's going on?" Skyler asked.

One of the red security officers put his hand out keeping Skyler from coming closer. "Cadet please stand back and let us do our job."

Skyler took a step back.

Michael called out. "Rob, what happened?"

Rob was now sitting in the back of the van. "They think I killed Nancy. They are taking me into questioning, nothing more than that."

Michael's eyes locked with Rob's. He could see his cold dark black soulless eyes looking back at him. "Did you do it?"

Rob nodded. "They don't have a body to say I did. You can thank me later Skyler."

Skyler stood there feeling awkward.

Michael put his hand on Skyler's shoulder. "I believe you have nothing to do with this, you know what Rob is like." Michael waved goodbye to Rob.

Skyler awkwardly waved goodbye to Rob.

Michael watched the security guards turn the laser net on before locking the doors.

Michael turned to Skyler after the van drove away. "Well I guess we found out what happened."

Skyler stood there dumbstruck. "I, in no way wanted her dead."

Michael sighed. "I believe you."

Chapter 40

Skyler walked into Cane's office. "Cane I need to ask you an important question."

Cane smiled. "Why so serious Skyler, please relax, take a seat and ask away?"

Skyler took a deep breath. "Why are the Cass attacking Earth and nowhere else?"

Cane frowned. "Who told you that they were just attacking Earth? That's not true many other planets and colonies are being attacked. Earth is the most dangerous of all of them, but we are not being singled out."

"Well, then why are the Cass at war what did we do to them to make them so angry to attack us?"

Shaking his head. "I have no idea, Skyler. I have not talked to them that is not my job and they refuse to talk or make a public statement. The only thing we have gotten back from them is a message that said, *You know why you deserve this, and we will make you pay till the wrong is right.* I don't know, and I have never known what that message was referring to. That came years ago back with the first war and they have not communicated with us since. The Cass that are on Earth they say they don't know, and they left because they wanted a different life so either this a very well-kept secret or it's nonsense."

Skyler sat down in the chair. "Well this makes little sense what did we ever do to the Cass?"

Cane shook his head. "Like I said I don't know. This is a puzzle to me as they have been fighting with us since before, I was born. But what I do know is we have no choice but to fight them, or they will just keep killing."

Skyler rubbed his face. "So, if they're going to war with us again my dad died for nothing?

Cane straightened in his seat and gave Skyler a dark glare. "What are you talking about. The Cass betrayed us. Your dad died saving his entire crew. He sacrificed himself for humanity. I know the Cass said they were at peace with us and lied and killed a few more thousand humans, but that had nothing to do with your father. He was a hero."

Skyler took a deep sigh and looked down at his feet.

Cane knew something was off with him. "Skyler, what is really bugging you? I'm not a trained therapist, but I can do my best."

Skyler shook his head. He didn't want to talk, but he knew it was all for the best. "Well, sir it's everything that has happened this year and what is going to happen next year. Next year I will be a fourth year and Kax is a fifth and Michael sixth. You have helped Michael a lot by keeping him off the frontlines, but he is still at risk. Kax could graduate. Everything I know is changing. I want to stay in for the full seven years but if this war gets worse-"

Cane cut him off. "Is that all you are worried about?"

Skyler shook his head. "No sir the list goes on."

Cane let out a deep sigh. "Michael will not be sent to frontlines. I have put him on special assignments. There is a list of job options Kax can pick from on the list that has been sent to her. Now when it comes to you, I can give you a list of options, but I think the safest and best thing to do would be to leave Earth right now and that's what your doing."

Skyler took a deep breath. "What about my friends? Will these new career options take me away from my friends?"

Cane typed in a few things on his computer, "I have sent you an e-mail with the options you have for your career. And I have sent Michael and Kax their own set. If you three do really want to stay, I'd talk to each other about your options. In this line of work friends are important. It can be lonely in space; you need someone by your side."